THE
LIGHTKEEPER

To Chris —
Happy reading !
Linda DuVal

THE
LIGHTKEEPER

LINDA DUVAL

East of the Mountains  and West of the Sun™

RHYOLITE PRESS LLC
Colorado Springs, Colorado

DuVal, Linda
The Lightkeeper / Linda DuVal
First edition, January 1, 2024

ISBN 978-1-943829-53-8

Library of Congress Control Number: 2023949898

Published in the United States of America
by Rhyolite Press LLC
P.O. Box 60144
Colorado Springs, Colorado 80960
www.rhyolitepress.com

Cover design, book design and layout by Donald Kallaus

*To my mother, who died in
2022, and who loved to tell—
and read—a good story.*

CHAPTER ONE

A top the lighthouse's pinnacle, Amy Pritchard watched as the stars were consumed by angry ebony clouds, crawling across the sky like an inky octopus. A storm was coming. A shiver ran up her arms and she rubbed them absent-mindedly. Her long dark hair, unbound, whipped around her lean body like a tattered cloak.

She secretly loved the storms. They were exciting and made her feel alive—even if it was for just a little bit.

As the lightkeeper on Point Peril, she had experienced a number of them in recent months. The cracking thunder, brilliant flashes of lightning and towering waves scared her little. They thrilled her. And they distracted her from her grief.

Amy's husband, Reuben Pritchard, had died in the Civil War. She never knew quite how, or when, or exactly where. His body rested, most certainly, in an unmarked and untended grave somewhere in the Deep South.

Reuben had been a handsome fellow, quite the catch her parents said, heir to the saw mill in her hometown. He was not unkind, but not overly demonstrative, either. He rarely offered a compliment, but neither was he free with criticism. He had, in his reserved way, seemed to love her. And he openly adored their daughter, Rebecca, who was only two years old when he went off to fight for the Union, only three when he went missing. The dark-haired, dark-eyed child had charmed everyone who met her, including her rather stern father.

Faced with raising a child on her own, Amy moved back into her parents' New England home while she observed her widowhood and figured out what to do next. James and Margaret Bennett were more than happy to have their daughter home, in their care, despite the circumstances.

Rebecca was the only bright spot in Amy's life. Taking care of her, teaching her, playing with her, reading to her—those things filled Amy's days. It was only at night that she fought the loneliness and felt useless, a guest in her parents' household. She struggled with what to do with herself, now that she didn't have a household of her own to tend. Being a wife and mother had filled her existence for the past few years. She had actually liked housework and, with the help of a cook/housekeeper, had done most things herself. Except cooking, of which she was never fond.

Her parents suggested that she might marry again—but Amy had neither the inclination nor desire to pursue that condition yet. She felt like she was in some sort of limbo. Only Rebecca gave her joy.

When she was four, Rebecca caught a fever and though Amy and her mother spent countless hours nursing her. Amy could only watch helplessly as her lively little daughter faded from life.

Amy was bereft, inconsolable in her grief. She spent weeks alone in her room, eating little and crying till her eyes were swollen shut. Her mother would come in and brush her long, dark hair, talk softly to her and try to get her to leave the room.

"You must get on with your life," she told her daughter repeatedly.

But Amy could not face a world without her young family, and though she missed Reuben, it was her daughter's death that left her most desolate. She thought more than once about just walking into the surf near her parents' sea-side home and letting the ocean claim her sorrow.

Always somewhat shy and reserved, as an only child Amy had long since turned inward when things upset her. Books, her lifetime source of escape, did not even interest her right now. Numbness enslaved her, body, soul and mind. Weeks became months.

One night, her parents invited a business associate of her father's—another banker from a nearby town—to come to dinner. They kindly but insistently encouraged Amy to join them at the meal, and she finally relented. She found that all of her clothes hung on her tall, and now thinner, frame like wash on a clothesline. But she managed to find a sash to belt one of her smaller garments, fashioned her waist-length dark hair into a simple plait, and made it downstairs for the repast.

The banker—a stout, bearded and well-traveled fellow— chatted with her father about banking, which Amy was able to ignore. Then he said something that caught her attention. He was talking about the shortage of men to do certain jobs since the war had ended. He'd even had to hire and train women to be tellers at his bank, he said. One of the other jobs now going to women, he said in amazement, was the task of lighthouse keepers.

"I guess even a woman can keep a light burning," he joked. It was the first thing that had piqued Amy's interest for months. Her head, heretofore bowed over her plate, came up.

She looked around and realized she had not been seeing faces for a long time. Her parents had aged! Well, of course, they had lost their only granddaughter, as well as their son-in-law, and almost (they had worried) their daughter.

Amy was struck with a deep sense of shame, an uncomfortable warmth curling in her chest. She had been so selfish. Guilt impelled her to stiffen her spine and she asked quietly: "So… how does a woman become a lighthouse keeper?"

HER FATHER TRIED to bribe her to stay.

"If it's work you want, I can let you do some filing at the bank," he offered. "You always were good with numbers. Maybe you can even become a teller."

For once, Amy held her ground with her parents. She was a widow now, and needed to make her own way in the world. Something about being stationed at a remote lighthouse appealed to her strongly at this point in her life.

Not long after that fateful dinner, she applied for the position. She was then scheduled for an interview with a Captain Parker of the Lighthouse Service, and her father insisted on accompanying her. She didn't care. He wasn't talking her out of it. The more she thought about it, the more she wanted this job.

Captain Parker looked askance at her when she entered his office for the interview. He eyed her tall, slender figure and pale cheeks and, knowing she was the daughter of gentry, worried that she might be too frail for this job. Most of the women he had hired were more robust, used to hard work. But he interviewed her anyway, as a courtesy.

He began his inquisition.

He asked things like "Can you climb four flights of stairs? Can you carry a bucket of water in each hand? Can you cook and care for yourself? Can you manage to stay awake all night if needed?"

Amy answered in the affirmative, quietly but determinedly, to each query. She believed she could do all those things. She'd have to learn to cook, though. He didn't need to know that.

"I have always been strong—for a woman," she told him, meeting his eyes for the first time. He saw a resolve there that surprised him. And a grief that did not. He knew her story.

One question was: "Can you row a boat?" Amy hedged on that question. She and a girlfriend had rowed a boat once—awkwardly, at best—around a small lake one time. But she felt like she needed to say yes, so she did.

She was warned that the job would begin on a trial basis, and that the position might last just a few months, or possibly a few years, till a man could be found to replace her. She'd deal with that when the time came, she thought.

After weeks of waiting, she finally received a letter telling her she was hired on a trial basis and could begin as soon as the paperwork was complete and she was packed and ready.

Two months later, on a misty, gray May morning, Amy rode with her father in a carriage behind a horse-drawn dray filled with the meager belongings she had chosen to bring—a rope bed, a sturdy rocking chair and a small writing desk she had loved since she was a schoolgirl. There also was a carved chest of drawers Reuben had bought her as a wedding gift. A modest-sized trunk held her clothes. She had left behind all her best dresses, figuring she would little need them in a lighthouse.

Her worried parents had argued with her about the move until the day she departed their home.

"It'll be hard work," her father warned. "You've never done labor like this."

Amy welcomed the thought—if she worked hard enough, got tired enough, she might actually sleep without nightmares.

"You'll be so isolated, so lonely," her mother had said. The first appealed to Amy, and the second was true anyway.

Now, as they drove through the small harbor town of Port Smythe—named for founder Ambrose Smythe—she saw a few small shops but took little notice of them. There also was a general store, a blacksmith shop and livery stable, an inn and a quaint steepled church, plus a scattering of houses along narrow streets. She didn't intend to spend much time here. They drove past the port for which the town got half of its name. Not large, but bustling.

The road from town ran along the headland to the cliff, a mile away, where the lighthouse stood sentinel. She would be able to see the town from the lighthouse, and vice versa, she imagined.

Finally, they arrived at Point Peril. The tall white lighthouse was snugged up against a small stone cottage—where presumably she would live. The burly dray driver pulled his draft horse to a halt and climbed down. He had been paid to unload the wagon.

Sitting up on a large rock next to the lighthouse was a gnome of a man, a sturdy wooden wheelbarrow at his feet.

He sprung down with an agility that belied his age. His shaggy salt-and-pepper hair was tucked partly beneath a fisherman's cap and his clothes flapped around him like a scarecrow's. A small, wiry frame indicated a man who worked hard and walked a lot.

"Charlie Jenkins, pleased to meetcha," he said, extending his hand to Amy's father. He did a funny little bow to Amy.

"Welcome ter Point Peril," he added. "I'll be yer pervisioner."

Pervisioner? Amy suppressed a small smile.

"And just what provisions do you intend to provide?" she asked, politely.

Charlie said he would come every week with meat, some vegetables, and staples such as flour, sugar and salt.

"And me wife, Bess, and me owns a cow. Daisy produces way more than we can use, so I'll throw in some milk and butter, too," he said.

Amy watched the drayman unload her furniture. She was anxious to see the inside of the cottage. After all, it was going to be her home.

Charlie could see her distraction, so he grabbed his wheelbarrow, promised to be back later "ter show yer the way of things" and gave her a nod before striking out down the lighthouse road with his rather odd gait. The wheelbarrow almost seemed to be an extension of his arms.

Amy turned her attention to the cottage. It was small but solid, built from local white stone, and not unattractive. A few flowers out front might help make it more cheerful, she thought.

She entered the cottage door, just a few steps away from the lighthouse door, and stopped to take it all in. The cool, austere interior was mostly one room. A kitchen area with an iron cook-stove stood at one end, beneath a small window overlooking the ocean. A stone sink was nearby, and featured a pump handle that meant she had access to water inside the house. A wooden cupboard for staples and a worn wooden table with three chairs completed that part of the room.

The drayman was setting up her rope bed on the far corner of the room, lacing the rope back and forth on the hooks attached to the frame. A featherbed would go on top of that. He had put it near a door that led to a water closet. My, my, indoor plumbing of sorts, she thought (though she had spotted an outhouse behind some bushes not too far from the cottage). A metal washtub hung on the wall outside the water closet — presumably for laundry and also for bathing, though not all of one's body at a time.

A small stone fireplace along one wall was the perfect place for her rocking chair. She wouldn't be having company. The cottage was somewhat chilly, but she could start a fire and warm things up before evening. She had seen some cut firewood outside the cottage, on the side away from the lighthouse.

It was everything she needed. Solitude, if not solace.

CHAPTER TWO

Amy's father seemed at a loss for words. He chatted nervously —totally unlike him—and fussed over small things until Amy took him by the hands and told him it was all right to leave. He seemed both unsure and relieved. Good-byes were hard, especially in such a foreign situation. She had never lived more than a stone's throw away from her parents. Now, they were half a day's ride away. Finally, he left, waving good-bye every few yards down the road as he departed.

Her father had not been gone long when Charlie returned to give her instructions. Normally, he told her, repeating the story she now knew, a military man would be posted at the lighthouse, but a shortage of men after the war meant some civilians, including women, had been hired for the job. Spinsters and widows were preferred, he said, because they didn't have the distractions of children or husbands and they "mostly didn't take ter the drink" like men.

The lighthouse was perched on a cliff overlooking the ocean, on a jut of land that seemed perfect for such a purpose The cliff face directly in front of the lighthouse was sheer and rocky. But on one side of the summit, the landscape sloped away to a set of wide stone stairs that led to the sandy beach below. Banks of sea roses flanked the seawall and were just in bud. They might be pretty when they bloomed, she thought. The terrain on the other side of the lighthouse, where the cottage stood, sloped more gradually and a well-worn path ran along the top of the cliff face.

Amy entered the lighthouse itself and looked around at the near-empty interior.

"Is the light on top?" she asked, peering upward.

"It's called the lamp, not the light," Charlie informed Amy, and commenced showing her how to maintain the lighthouse. He had once been the lightkeeper himself, he told her, and had "filled in" since the last one left and she had arrived. They climbed the wrought iron stairs to the third level, which he called the "watch" level and she could see far out to sea through the ocean-facing windows here.

"How close do ships have to be to see the light?" she asked, timidly.

"I s'pect they can see it twenty miles or more," he replied, pleased she had asked him a question finally.

He kept glancing at her, as if wondering if she were up to the job, but he didn't say so.

They then ascended to the top or "light" level, completely surrounded by thick glass panes and where most of her work would be done. Catwalks surrounded each of the top two levels, to allow outside access so she could clean the windows regularly. Ah, this is where the question about two buckets of water came in. One for cleaning, one for rinsing, she guessed. Charlie confirmed her suspicions.

She thought she might get dizzy on these windy catwalks, but she found she rather enjoyed being up there. Charlie turned her attention to the lamp itself.

"We use'ter use whale oil, but now we use lard oil," he explained, showing her how to care for the wick and clean the lens. "I hears some of 'em use kerosene now, but not us." he added. "Mebbe someday."

Charlie also explained that the nation had lighthouse districts and that each one was run by a naval officer appointed by the Lighthouse Board to be the district inspector. Theirs was a Lieutenant John Sparks.

"He'll be 'round one of these days to check on yer," Charlie promised.

As they descended the 55 steps to the bottom, Amy realized she was going to have to hem her skirts so she would not trip on the steep, curving stairs. A fall would be painful, if not fatal. Oh, well, sewing would give her something to do. And she certainly wasn't worried about being fashionable.

Charlie left her with enough "pervisions" to last her a week and promised to return to check on her.

"I can see the light from me own cottage," he said. "So I'll know if yer havin' troubles."

His own place, he told her, was about half a mile farther along the headland, where the well-worn path led. She could barely see his cottage, but it was a comfort to know it was there. And she would be getting that visit from that Lieutenant Sparks.

Amy wasn't sure if Charlie's comment about Sparks' visit was a veiled threat or meant as reassurance. She really didn't care. She knew she could do the job the old man described and that if she did it well, she might be left alone. And that was what she wanted.

Just seven months after Rebecca's death, her grief was still raw, and talking to others was still a chore. Feeling anything, even friendliness or empathy, was beyond her right now. Still, she couldn't just sit in her rocking chair by the fire and wish the days away. Here, there was much to do.

For the first time in a long time, she found herself planning what had to be done and in what order. It was a welcome distraction from wallowing in self-pity, which is what she suspected she had been doing.

Reading the instructions she had been given when she got the job, Amy knew there was a lot of work involved. She had to light the lamp at sunset every night and keep it bright until sunrise. The wicks needed to be trimmed regularly and evenly. The lamps and reflectors needed to be kept clean and polished with a special powder and leather rags.

She was expected to keep a daily journal of observations about the weather and regularly record the barometric pressure indicated on the barometer in the lighthouse. She also needed to note the temperature and whether or not it had rained. All this would keep her busy—but not busy enough.

Amy decided she would ask Charlie about getting seeds and seedlings for a garden. Just a few things: carrots, onions, potatoes, peas, cabbage and maybe some pole beans. She'd have to prepare the soil first. Being May, the coldest part of the spring was likely past, so she could plant at any time. At home, she had loved to work in the garden with their gardener, Amos Avery, ever since she was a child. She knew a bit about it, though she wished now she had paid closer attention to his instruction. Her favorite part of gardening had been sitting the in the soft dirt, eating raw, fresh-shelled peas or sun-warmed strawberries.

Her mother had scolded her, telling her it was "unladylike."

Amy went inside the cottage. Its cool darkness would

be welcome in the summer, she thought. The thick glazed windows didn't let in a lot of light, though. She might have to sit outdoors in the sunlight to see well enough to hem her skirts.

She swept the cottage floor with an old, worn broom (she was making a list of things she might need to buy) and made her bed with a favorite quilt once used on Rebecca's bed. She caressed the lovingly worn red-and-white starburst pattern. Made by her mother years ago, it had been her own favorite as a child and then Rebecca's favorite. It did add a spot of brightness to the dim cottage. As she touched the quilt, she could picture Rebecca's sweet face looking up from the pillow, waiting for a goodnight kiss. Amy's eyes filled with tears. She didn't think she had any left, but there they were again.

She shook herself and rose, went outside to gather firewood, and returned to start a small blaze in the fireplace. The chimney drew well—that was a relief.

She decided to have a simple meal and eat early, then go to bed with the sun. She was tired. Charlie's wife, Bess, had sent a crock of soup and a chunk of homemade brown bread for her supper, "since yer prob'ly need to get settled" and might not be up for cooking. She was grateful and would be sure to tell Charlie so when he returned.

After she ate and cleaned her dishes with water heated on the stove—which Charlie had thoughtfully stoked for her—Amy went outside to sit on the seawall, smell the salt air and watch the ocean. It was calm tonight, and the soft swells kissing the shore so gently made her feel calm, too, and eventually sleepy.

Yes, she thought, this would do.

. . .

AMY SOON DISCOVERED she really wasn't a very good cook. At home, growing up, they had a cook—which as a child she had predictably dubbed Cookie—and Amy's cooking had been limited mostly to scones and fancy sandwiches for her mother's teas, an occasional dessert, such as a syllabub, and perhaps a salad if she felt like a lunch lighter than what her parents preferred for the midday meal.

Her cook/housekeeper after she was married was a better housekeeper than cook, but her simple meals had suited Reuben fine, so Amy was content, too. Now she began to realize how hard the task really was.

After burning two batches of biscuits, she finally got it right. The stove had a perverse personality all its own and she took to calling it Beelzebub. She even kicked it a few times. Growing up an only child who sought out adults for companionship, she had sat on a kitchen stool and watched Cookie make enough soups and stews that she finally got the hang of that, too.

A small root cellar behind the cottage showed signs of mice, so she stored most of her perishables in the base of the lighthouse, which was secure and stayed cool all summer. Eggs and milk and leftover stew kept well there in stone crocks. She ate simply and found that planting a garden and tending the lighthouse had improved her appetite.

Every night, she sat in her rocking chair and brushed out her hair till it shone. Come morning, it went back into its simple plait, which was much easier to manage when doing her chores.

Charlie Jenkins came every few days, not weekly as he had first said. Amy suspected he was either checking up on her or worried about her. She didn't take offense.

One day, he caught her on her knees in the garden, picking out stones and weeds to make the cultivation easier. He watched her for a moment, then set down his wheelbarrow.

"Yer ever garden afore?" he asked, scratching his head.

"Not really," she replied. "I've planted some flowers but have never grown vegetables on my own." She sat back on her heels, admiring her work.

"Well, then, yer might want ter know yer just pulled up three cabbage plants," he said. And he proceeded to show her how to identify weeds from vegetables. Amy was amazed to see how different little baby cabbage plants looked compared to the grown ones.

Learning new things and figuring out how to be self-sufficient was helping her cope. The crushingly sad moments came less often. When she lay awake at night, her thoughts were more on the chores she had waiting for her in the morning, and less on the losses she had borne.

One morning, after a stormy night, the ocean was a little wild and Amy glanced at the foamy surf as she walked along the seawall. In the white surf, she saw a dark head appear.

Amy froze. Someone was out there! Maybe drowning! What should she do? She didn't know how to swim, but found herself racing down the wide stone steps to the beach. Panic rose in her like she was drowning herself. She looked around for something—anything—that might float.

When she looked back at the roiling surf, she realized there were several dark heads bobbing in and out of the waves. Then she heard the barks.

Seals! She hadn't seen any for years, but there they were, playing in the waves, diving and surfacing. Now that she could hear them, their joyous barks were a familiar and comforting sound from her childhood.

She sank to her knees in relief. Then she sat and watched them as they frolicked in the rough water, happy to be tossed about like life preservers. She came to watch for them every day that summer and they got so used to her slim figure perched on a rock by the shore, they stopped being wary of her. She loved watching them, and had a thought: Should I learn to swim, too?

So the next day, she put on her oldest camisole and bloomers, immodestly revealing her bare arms and her legs to the knees and waded into the incoming breakers. She gradually got braver and went in all the way to her neck, but no deeper than that. She felt her body bob up with each swell of the ocean.

She had seen people swim, so she copied what she thought were swimming movements. At first, she sank like a stone. Swallowed a bit of sea water. Then she began to dog paddle and got good enough that she could "swim" parallel from the big rock to the pile of driftwood on shore. The ocean was cool, so she didn't stay in very long, but she was secretly proud of her newfound skill.

Her secret didn't last long.

One June day, while cooling off in the salt water, she saw someone standing on the shore, watching her. As she crept closer to beach, embarrassed about her bathing costume, she realized with some relief that it was a woman.

A short, portly lady with gray hair and an apron stood there. As Amy waded ashore, the woman picked up an old sheet Amy was using to dry off after her dips, and wrapped it around the younger woman.

"Better not let Charlie see you doing that," the woman

scolded, mildly. "He worries about you as it is."

Amy shivered, pulled the sheet tighter, and held out her hand as politely and with as much dignity as if she were greeting guests for high tea.

"Amy Pritchard," she said. "How do you do?"

The woman took it, but instead of shaking it, patted it and gave it a squeeze.

"I'm Bess, Charlie's wife," she replied. "And there's no doubt as to who you are. Charlie described you perfectly.

"I've brought you a few things," the woman said. She held open a basket, revealing a meat pie, some slices of roast pork, a cake and a jar of pickles, among other things.

"Come up to the cottage," Amy invited her, and they climbed the stone steps to the top of the seawall.

Inside the cottage, Amy excused herself and went into the tiny water closet to change. It was awkward, but she managed.

When she came out, Bess was making tea on the evil stove.

"I brought some honey cake," Bess said, and waved to the table where it sat, wrapped in a cloth. "Wanted to meet you sooner. But I've been occupied some, helping my youngest daughter with her first baby. She's had some troubles."

Bess' pleasant face and soft blue eyes reminded Amy of Cookie, and she took an instant liking to the woman.

"Thank you," Amy said, and sat down, suddenly feeling like a guest in her own home. Bess cut slices of the cake and served them.

"Charlie has been my lifeline," Amy said. "And I am glad to thank you personally for the wonderful food. I'm afraid I'm not a great cook."

Amy took a bite of the cake. It was ambrosia, a buttery

confection studded with dried fruits and nuts.

"'S wonderful!" Amy said, mouth full, forgetting her manners.

Bess laughed.

"I'm glad you like it," she said, pouring them tea. She seemed to know where everything was.

"Do you mind if I ask you a question? I'm dying of curiosity!" Bess said.

Amy hesitated for a moment.

"Yes, go ahead," she said, swallowing her last bite of cake and impolitely licking her fingers.

"Why would a lovely young woman like yourself be willing to take on a lonely job like this?"

Amy tensed, felt the tears begin to well in her eyes and tried to control them. It was no use. And it wasn't just a few tears. She began to shake with sobs.

Bess swiftly rose from her seat and rushed around the table to hug Amy.

"I'm so sorry!" she said. "I'm just a nosy old woman. Forget I asked!"

Amy shook her head and wiped her eyes. Then she took a deep breath and began to talk—about Reuben, about Rebecca, about her grief. It came pouring out. She had never talked to a stranger like this in her whole life, but it seemed natural to tell this kind woman.

When she was finished, Bess hugged her again and was silent for a while.

"Well, this might be just what you need, being a lightkeeper and all," Bess said. "It'll give you time to heal."

After Amy composed herself, and they drank more tea, they talked of other things. Amy told Bess about her childhood home and her parents and about how she got the job. Bess explained why she was so familiar with the cottage.

"Charlie and me used to be the caretakers here," Bess said. "Then he got too old to climb them stairs with two buckets of water. Had to do one at a time. Finally, decided to give it up to become the provisioner instead."

She showed Amy a few tricks about taming Beelzebub. She looked around the cottage and decided it needed another rocking chair, in case Amy had visitors.

"I have one in the attic I'm not using, so if you want it, I'll make a fresh cushion for it, and have Charlie bring it over," she said.

They looked at the garden and she offered Amy a few tips on growing vegetables.

"You need to thin out them puny ones to let the healthy ones grow," she said, looking at the carrots.

Amy thanked her for everything and found that when the woman left, she was alone again, but not as lonely as she had been before.

REALIZING THAT SHE HAD SEEN NO ONE but Charlie and Bess since she arrived, Amy decided to go to the charming little church in town one Sabbath. She put on the best thing she had—a plain black skirt that hadn't been shortened for work, and a crisp white shirtwaist—and headed into town one fair summer Sunday morning. She could hear the church bell peal as she walked down the stony road toward town.

It was such a lovely day, she thought perhaps she'd just skip church and keep walking, but as she drew closer, realized that it would be too obvious to walk on by when everyone else was headed into the service.

Inside, it was stuffy and warm, with sun piercing the small stained-glass windows. She took a seat in the rear of the church and waited for the service to begin. A fly buzzing at one of the windows made a low droning hum and she began to drift off. She caught her breach of manners and made herself stay awake. She noticed the curious side glances of the town folk, who had undoubtedly heard about the widow-lady lightkeeper on Point Peril.

The service was fairly boring, except for the singing, which Amy liked, and the minister was a bit of a drone but not a fire-breather, which suited her just fine. When it was over, he was waiting outside to greet his flock. Amy hung back, hoping he would go before she emerged, but had no such luck.

"Good morning!" he said, offering her a short, formal bow when she finally emerged. "We meet at last. I'm the Reverend Jonathan Snead. At your service."

His clothes were fine, but not ostentatious, and his light brown eyes matched his thinning light brown hair. He was average height—no taller than she—and had just a hint of a paunch on his otherwise slim frame. He seemed innocuous enough, but something about him was off-putting, she thought.

"Nice to meet you," she replied with a hint of a curtsey, and introduced herself. "It's a sweet little church."

"Yes," he said. "A bit small to my liking, but I'll be on to bigger and better things one of these days. And you can't second-guess the Lord about his plans for you." Privately, she suspected the Reverend Snead second-guessed the Lord a lot.

Ah, yes, he was one of those ambitious types, she thought.

"May I walk you home?" he asked. "It's a fine day and I

could use with a bit of exercise."

Amy didn't want to talk to him any longer, so she begged off, saying she was going to stop by and visit Bess and Charlie before going home. But she thanked him politely. Then she went straight home.

As she walked toward the lighthouse and Point Peril, she felt a little flutter in her stomach, like the feeling she had as a child when her father's carriage neared home.

She realized the little lighthouse cottage had already become home to her. As she came around the last bend in the road, she saw her mother standing on the cottage stoop, waiting for her.

"We didn't know where you were!" her mother said, and rushed forward to hug her in greeting. "We were getting worried. Your father went down to the beach to see if you were around."

Well, this was unexpected. Her parents had driven hours to get here—with no warning—and faced hours more on the road home. Amy suddenly appreciated the effort they had made.

"I'm so glad to see you," Amy said, hugging her mother. "I was only gone for a bit, to Sunday service. Come inside."

Her mother tried to hide her disappointment at the interior with its two mismatched rocking chairs and its primitive water closet. Amy became defensive.

"Mother, it's all I need," she said, putting on water for tea. She was relieved when her father showed up at the door and entered, changing the tone of the conversation.

"Well, well," he said. "You've made it quite homey. And I see your garden is coming along."

Her mother stared at him, then her, in horror.

"You mean she does the gardening herself,"" she asked. "And who does the cooking and cleaning? I thought you said she had a servant."

Amy's father looked sheepish.

"I said she had someone to help her," he clarified.

Amy laughed. The sound startled her, it had been so long since she had laughed out loud.

"Charlie? Charlie is not a servant, but he does help me. He brings me everything I need to live here. But I serve myself. I cook for myself, I clean the house, I tend the garden. And I ...yes, I ... manage the lighthouse. What did you think a lightkeeper did? It's important work, keeping ships from running into the rocks offshore. And there are a lot of ships that pass here. I see their sails all the time."

She had become quite defensive, so she took a breath and tried to calm down. Her mother meant well, but she had seriously underestimated Amy's abilities.

She made her parents a lunch of salad with early greens from her garden and leftover chicken and dumplings. The second-day dumplings were a bit soggy. Her mother seemed grudgingly impressed, but picked at her food.

"Maybe you should come home for a week and take some lessons from Cookie," she said.

"I can't do that," Amy said. "I can't leave the lighthouse un-attended."

"Never?" her mother asked.

"Never," Amy said. "At least, not for more than a couple of hours and only during the day when the weather is fair."

When they left, Amy was relieved. Whatever her parents thought of her new life, it suited her just perfectly.

CHAPTER THREE

On another sunny day, when the lighthouse needed little tending for the morning, she set out early for Port Smythe on foot—her only option, really. She was a good rider, but she had no horse. She had a shopping list—short, but necessary. First of all, she needed a new broom. And a better frying pan. And a bucket that did not leak. So when she got to town, she headed for the general store, hoping to find the items she needed.

She entered the crowded, somewhat dark shop and stopped a moment to let her eyes adjust from the bright sunlight. Once again, she wore her "Sunday best" black skirt and white shirtwaist and had her hair in a neat braid.

When her eyes adjusted to the dim interior, she realized that everyone in the store was staring at her, some more obviously than others. It was a small town, and everyone probably knew everyone else. A stranger was something to be considered.

She forced a smile and went to the counter. The man there was a tall, skinny fellow with a shock of silver-gray hair and a mustache. He wore an apron and regarded her somewhat suspiciously.

"Hello," she said. "I'm Amy Pritchard, the lightkeeper at Point Peril. I'm glad to see you have such a good stock here at your shop. I need a few things, if you can help me."

"Ah," the shopkeeper said, smiling. "I'm Clyde Horton, proprietor. Pleased to meet you."

Amy held out her hand but Horton did not seem to know what to do with that, so she let it drop. She brought out the list of things she needed and he donned his spectacles to read it.

"Yes, yes, we can help you," he said, and scurried off to find the items she needed. Meanwhile, Amy looked around the store some more. There was a surprising array of household items, and she selected a packet of needles and some thread for shortening some more of her work skirts. She couldn't keep pinning them up forever, she thought.

Other women in the store eyed her surreptitiously, and finally an older woman with iron gray hair and a military bearing, aided by what Amy suspected was a formidable corset, approached her.

"Agatha Bean," she said, holding out her hand. Amy shook it. Agatha Bean had a very firm grip.

"Lightkeeper, eh?" Agatha Bean said. "Not a proper job for a woman, I would think. But if it suits you ..." She looked Amy up and down as if she were a horse for sale.

"Well, you're skinny, but I guess you look strong enough," she admitted. "So where's your husband."

Amy met the rude woman's eyes.

"He died," she said, bluntly, and with a jolt realized that was the first time she had said those words aloud. She briefly added, "Civil War."

Amy turned away before Agatha Bean could see the glisten of tears threatening to flood her eyes.

Mr. Horton was waiting for her at the counter with her things. Amy took a deep breath and approached him.

"How much do I owe you?" she asked, and counted out the money from her meager pay, which Charlie had delivered just the day before.

Then she gathered up her broom, bucket and frying pan, plus the needles and thread, and it made a very awkward package. But she was too proud to say so, and exited the store with the clumsy bundle.

As luck would have it, the Reverend Snead was driving past and he stopped his surrey. He tipped his hat.

"Need a ride home?" he offered.

Though she wasn't all that comfortable with the man, she figured he was a minister and he had transportation. Frankly, she wasn't sure she had given any thought to how she would get all these things home by herself.

"Thank you," she said, and he stepped down from the buggy to help her load her purchases.

On the way out to the lighthouse, he made small talk—mostly about himself—and when they arrived, he helped her unload the lot.

To be polite, she offered him tea for his trouble and he quickly accepted. She set about warming some scones from the day before and making a pot of tea. She dug out some of Bess' blackberry jam and presented him with an acceptable refreshment.

Snead bit into a scone and frowned.

"A bit dry," he said, wrinkling his nose.

Amy quickly apologized.

"I'm just learning to cook," she said, "and they're from

yesterday. I thought the jam would help. Mrs. Jenkins made it. It's quite delicious."

He nodded, his mouth full of dry scone and sweet jam. He washed it down with some tea into which he had spooned a copious amount of her precious sugar.

"A minister's wife must be a good cook," he pronounced, out of the blue. "You might want to work on that."

Amy wondered briefly why on earth he would say such a thing. Surely he wasn't suggesting …? But no. She dismissed his words. He was a prig, she decided. And she pitied any woman who married him.

She began to feel uncomfortable with him just sitting there, staring at her now that he had finished his tea. So she invited him out to see her garden.

He didn't seem impressed, but he did take her hand and hold it for a long time while he bade her farewell, mentioning that he had not seen her in church every Sunday but hoped her attendance would be more regular.

"A good Christian woman should attend church every Sabbath," he said.

"I can't always leave the lighthouse," Amy replied, only slightly stretching the truth.

"Ah, I see," he replied, then climbed into his surrey and left.

Amy was relieved to see him go. She could not wait to use her new broom and try out the frying pan.

The next morning, Charlie Jenkins came by with food-stuffs and a surprise: a round white life preserver. He left it in the lighthouse.

"I don't hold with yer swimmin' in the sea," he said, "but if yer got to do it, use that thing to keep from drownin'." Bess must have tattled on her.

The preserver had some writing on it, too faded to read. Amy assumed it came from a ship no longer in service, or perhaps one even shipwrecked on this very shore. The thought made her shiver.

After he left, Amy decided to try swimming with the object, but it kept her from stroking with her arms. Yes, it did keep her afloat, but it didn't do a thing for her learning to swim. She chucked it back into the base of the lighthouse with miscellaneous other things previous occupants had "stored" there.

One July day, a man came riding up the road to the lighthouse on a well-groomed chestnut gelding. He was in uniform and Amy correctly guessed that this was the long-promised visit from her supervisor, the elusive Lieutenant John Sparks.

She brushed the garden dirt off her skirt as best she could, wiped her hands on a cloth and smoothed back errant strands of hair into her braid before greeting him.

He rode up and sat there for a minute inspecting the lighthouse, the cottage and finally, Amy.

"Everything ship-shape?" he asked, without introducing himself.

"I think so," Amy replied, for the first time hesitant about her caretaking skills. "Would you like some tea?"

"First, a look around," he said, dismounting and dropping his reins to the ground, a practice known as ground-tying, where the best-trained horses took the dropped reins as a sign they were not to stray.

Sparks was above average height with black hair, graying at the temples. He had the build and the bearing that defined a military man.

He removed his riding gloves and entered the lighthouse before her. He examined the lamp and checked to see if the windows were clean, asked a few terse questions and then descended to the ground level.

"Tea?" she asked again. He turned his gray eyes to take her in. A quirk at the corner of his mouth might have been the beginnings of a smile.

"I hear from the locals that you're not the world's best cook," he said, though not unkindly. "I think I'll take my tea in town at the inn, but thank you. Everything looks good." With that, he mounted his horse and they trotted away.

Amy wasn't sure whether to be insulted or relieved. A little bit of both, maybe.

As summer began to wane, Amy noticed that the lush red-orange blooms of the sea roses gave way to fat rose hips—the fattest ones she had ever seen. They would make good tea and help keep her healthy during the coming fall and winter, she thought. If Cookie was right, that is.

Her garden was producing a bounty of lovely vegetables—some nights, she just had a plate of vegetables for dinner with some of Bess' fine butter and a bit of salt for seasoning.

One morning, she opened her front door to find a thin orange cat sitting on her doorstep. It trotted in and jumped up into one of her rocking chairs, turned around twice, then settled down and went sound asleep.

Amy just stood there with her mouth open. What on earth? Where had it come from? Why did it think her rocking chair was its bed? Then she laughed softly to herself. Another orphan, she supposed. Maybe it would clear the mice out of the root cellar so she could use it this winter.

The cat, which she named Matilda once she had identified it as a female, seemed right at home in the cottage and its surroundings, as if it had lived here before.

When Charlie came next, she asked him.

"One cat's the same ter me as the next," he said, "but it does look a bit familiar-like. Maybe it belonged ter the last lightkeeper, who moved away. Cat must'a came back. Cats likes their own territories, y'know."

So Matilda became Amy's companion. When she wanted to be petted or fed, she'd rub Amy's ankles. Other times, when Amy tried to pet her, she'd swat Amy's hand away as if to say, "Not now." She was, after all, a cat.

But it was company, company that she didn't have to entertain or talk to. That was ideal.

Matilda the cat did prove to be a good mouser, and fattened up on all the little pesky rodents within half a mile of the cottage. She could use the root cellar now, but she still liked to store most of her comestibles in the lighthouse. It seemed cleaner.

Charlie came loping down the path one September morning, wheelbarrow extension in front of him, with her weekly supplies.

"Yer'll be gettin' a wagonload of lard oil sometime this week, but not to worry," he said. "The draymen'll haul it up for yer."

It had been a calm summer, with just a spate of short-lived thunderstorms, and Amy had not had to spend many nights on watch in the lamp tower. Once she had the lamp set for the night, it pretty much did the trick.

"Looks ter be a stormy fall," Charlie predicted. "All the signs're there."

"What signs?" Amy asked, and was immediately sorry.

Charlie went on for about half an hour about caterpillar coats, how early the trees were turning, and the paths of the currents that ran past the point. Amy understood little of it, but admired his knowledge. It was the most she'd ever heard him speak at one time.

Her first real taste of the serious storm season came in mid-September, when a nor'easter blew in and raged around the little cottage. It was all she could do to walk the few steps from her front door to the lighthouse door. The fierce gale brought the waves almost up to the stone steps. She spent most of the night in the watch level, keeping an eye out for passing ships. She only saw one hardy vessel far out beyond the point, but she kept the lamp well lighted all night. The next day, she slept a good part of the morning and early afternoon. Sitting vigil was exhausting!

For all the hard work it took keeping the lighthouse ship-shape, as Lieutenant Sparks said, the job also had its unexpected joys.

She could climb the stairs and look out over the ocean any time she wanted, watching the passing ships, sometimes seeing whales breaching, and getting a bird's-eye-view of the playful seals.

One night, Amy dreamed she was in fairly calm water and the seals were frolicking all around her, but one dark head looked different from the others. She realized it was her Rebecca, playing in the surf with the creatures. She looked happy and she could swim as well as they could. She could even hear Rebecca's childish giggle.

Amy woke to find tears on her pillow, but something about the dream also made her happy. Her dreams seemed to be letting her come to terms with Rebecca's death. Before coming to Point Peril, she had only had nightmares.

Amy also discovered the joys of being barefoot.

She had never gone barefoot in her life. Not even as a child had she been allowed to go barefoot. Her mother, no doubt, thought it, too, was unladylike, or unsafe, or both.

She discovered it quite by accident. One day as she was walking along the beach, enjoying the sunshine and sea air, she stepped into a puddle because she was not looking where she was going. Her shoes got wet, and the damp leather became so uncomfortable, she took them off. And her wet stockings as well.

Oh, the feel of the sand between her toes was incredible. She flirted with the incoming tide and it flirted back. By the time she got home, her skirt was soaked to her knees, and she felt almost giddy with the freedom of being shoeless.

Then she discovered she could dart nimbly up the metal stairs of the lighthouse much faster in bare feet. On hot days, she even went about her housework and gardening barefoot.

She always kept her shoes nearby, lest she have an unexpected visitor and need to put them on quickly, so as not to shock anyone. It felt downright wicked to do these things— swim in the sea and run barefoot when she wanted. It felt like freedom.

ON A MUGGY OCTOBER DAY, unseasonably warm and suffocating, Amy walked on the beach, collecting a few shells, hair flying loose like a flag in the wind, trying to cool off. The waves were rough today, and the sky was ominous. Dark, low clouds were already beginning to build and she heard thunder rumble far out to sea.

She'd be awake all night tonight, she was pretty sure. She

probably should try to take a nap this afternoon, if she could. Maybe in the rocking chair. Matilda liked it when Amy sat in her rocker because Matilda liked to be rocked. She'd sit on Amy's lap for hours that way, if she could.

Toward evening, the wind became fiercer and quite chilly, so Amy built a fire in the cottage, re-braided her hair, made a stew she could keep for several meals and checked to make sure everything in the lighthouse was ready for a storm.

When Amy visited the light level and stood on the pinnacle, she realized this storm was going to be a bad one. In her six months here, she had not seen or felt one quite this ominous. Still, it was exciting.

Then, about midnight, all hell broke loose. The wind rose to a fever pitch, raging around the little cottage and lighthouse like a snarling beast. It plucked at every door and window, as if seeking entry.

When she went up to the watch level just after midnight, she strained her eyes to see if there were any ships foolish enough to brave the storm.

To her horror, there was one!

Not far from the rocks for which Point Peril was presumably named, a small ship was being tossed about on the violent waves. As she watched, a bolt of lightning struck one of the masts and she could see it collapse into the water. The ship seemed helpless as it was driven toward the rocks. Amy felt equally helpless as she watched it hit the rocks, shudder, then begin to sink.

She didn't know what to do. There was no way to summon help for the hapless sailors on board. All she could do was watch. There was no way to row a boat out to them in this violent turmoil. She wasn't sure how long she stood there, hands to mouth, praying for the poor souls who had been dashed into the roiling sea.

Then she saw something closer to shore—it looked like one of her seals, playing in the surf. But no, this creature was not a seal, and it was not playing. It was a man. And he was drowning.

Without another thought, she darted down the lighthouse stairs, dropped her skirt and spotted the abandoned life preserver resting near the door. She grabbed it, and ran, shucking her shawl and unbuttoning her blouse as she raced down the stone steps of the sea wall to the beach.

She waded into the rough waves, which pushed her back violently. But she had become stronger from her daily walks, her secret swims and from running up and down the lighthouse stairs. She forged ahead, into the water, which was shockingly icy tonight. She looked for the head she had seen appear above the waves, looked back at the lighthouse to orient herself, then shifted her gaze farther to her right.

There! She thought she saw a man's head rise above the water briefly, and she aimed in that direction. She used her awkward swimming skills and was glad of the life preserver this once.

Suddenly, a firm hand latched onto her braid. It pulled her under for a moment, and she tried not to swallow any sea water. Coughing, she surfaced, still clinging to the life preserver. The grip on her braid was gone. She frantically felt around her till she grasped what might be a man's shirt. She pulled with all her might, her muscles screaming, and his head came up close to hers. She slid the life preserver toward him and he was aware enough to grab for it instead of her braid.

"Hold on!" she yelled above the roar of the sea. She began to tow him toward the beach, but it was no easy task. The waves kept snatching her back, then shoving her down, then lifting her up so high she was afraid the exhausted sailor would lose his grip and she'd have to go after him again.

Finally, after an eternity of struggling, she felt sand beneath her bare toes. She dug in and pushed. Again. And again. And again. At last, they both lay, spent, on the cold, wet beach.

Once she regained her breath, Amy urged the man to stand and help her get him to the stone steps. One goal at a time, she thought.

He staggered and his knees kept buckling, but they finally got there. They rested again. Then she got him to crawl and practically pushed him from behind up the rain-slick steps, decorum be damned. They finally made it to the top. Amy was shaking with the effort and cripplingly cold by now, as was her charge.

Somehow, he managed to stand with her help and they staggered awkwardly to the cottage door. He nearly fell when they got through the door, but she used the momentum to guide him to the bed, where he collapsed.

Both were nearly immobile with the cold and the effort. Amy's teeth were chattering so hard, she was afraid her jaw would break. Her arms felt locked in a bent position.

She collapsed into her rocker and sat for a moment to gather her wits. What to do?

She couldn't help this man in her current state, so she went into the tiny water closet and stripped off her bloomers and camisole. Her stiff muscles felt frozen and it was not easy to remove the wet things. Her fingers were numb and she shook so hard, she could barely undo buttons and laces.

Finally, she got them off, and put on her warmest flannel nightgown, her wool winter robe and slippers.

The sailor was lying on her bed, still wet and shivering violently, but seemingly unconscious. She didn't have a choice. She began to strip off his wet clothes, too, and found dry bedding to replace what had gotten damp.

She rolled him to one side, then the other, to remove and replace the bedding. The effort left her sweating, if still cold. It was an odd sensation. He was a large man, and moving him without his help was a laborious task. Luckily, she had become strong from the rigors of her new lifestyle.

He seemed to regain a bit of awareness.

"C-c-c-cold," he said. A huge shudder shook his body. Amy realized that if he was even half as cold as she was, he must be nearly frigid. He had been in the water longer and had no exertion afterwards to get things warmed up again.

She built up the fire and stood by it, getting herself as warm as she could. She opened her robe to absorb the fire's warmth. She was still chilled to the bone, but the surface heat felt good. The flannel gown was deliciously hot against her skin.

Then she had a thought. She climbed into bed beside the sailor and used that surface heat to help warm him. He was out of his head and would never remember this, and it was the only way she could think of to quickly restore some heat to the poor fellow.

He kept shivering for a while, then began to calm. Amy felt some warmth return to her own limbs and before she knew it, she was asleep.

. . .

IT FELT LIKE BUTTERFLIES were fluttering across her skin. She'd never felt anything like it. As Amy began to rouse from her sleep, the room was still dark. Soft caresses covered her body. It took her a moment to realize she was still in bed with the drowning sailor. It was his hands, fluttering across her body lightly, testing, exploring in a tender fashion.

She went still. Somehow, her nightgown was up around her neck and shoulders. She should leap out of the bed and escape his attentions. But it felt so good to be stroked in this gentle way when she had not experienced human touch for so long. Or maybe it was the reaction to the terror and excitement of nearly dying in the ocean. It didn't matter. She felt lethargic from the efforts of the night, yet she was responding to this unexplained phenomenon. Soon, her nightgown was on the floor.

Then he kissed her, also gently, cautiously. Things escalated from there. She had never been touched like this, or kissed like this, and she could not stop herself from responding.

She had heard it called lovemaking, but had never experienced it this way. When it was over, the sailor wrapped his arms firmly around her and snugged her to him, then fell asleep. Exhausted, Amy did, too.

As the faint light of morning began to creep into the cottage, Amy awoke.

Horrified at what she had allowed to happen, she extricated herself carefully from the man's embrace and slipped out of bed. She hurried to the water closet and dressed.

What had she done? What had possessed her?

She paused. But who would ever know?

She made tea and toasted some bread from a stale loaf, buttered it and ate. She was sore from the night's exertions—

in the sea and beyond—but she felt good otherwise.

The sailor began to stir. The glow from the firelight allowed her a better look at him and she realized he was quite handsome, with hair a color she had never seen before. It was like burnished copper, now that it was dry. She dreaded the moment he opened his eyes, facing what they had done in the night.

She needn't have feared.

She sat in the rocking chair, brushing the seaweed and snarls out of her long tresses, when she heard a soft moan, and the sailor's eyelids fluttered.

"Mermaid," she thought she heard him mutter. He closed his eyes again and fell back into a deep sleep—or unconsciousness.

The storm, which had eased for a bit at dawn, once again raged outside. There would be no respite today. She finally donned her coat and scarf and braved the elements for that few seconds between cottage door and lighthouse door. She found her abandoned skirt on the floor, along with her shoes. She knew the rest of her clothing was lying, sodden, somewhere between lighthouse and beach. She'd get those things later.

She went up to check on the lamp and returned to the cottage. Her sailor was feverish and restless. She made him some rose hip tea and used a spoon to get him to swallow a bit once it cooled. He was only semi-conscious, and barely opened his eyes during her ministrations. His breathing became rough and irregular.

She didn't know how to care for someone this ill—her last attempt, with her own daughter, had failed. Then, with a shock, she realized that Rebecca had died just a year ago today. Tears welled in her eyes, but she brushed them away. She had an imminent problem that demanded her attention.

Should she try to get help? Dare she leave him alone?

For a few hours, she sponged his feverish body and kept giving him spoonsful of tea. She was still exhausted from the night before and when she wrapped herself in Rebecca's quilt and sat in the rocking chair, she fell asleep again.

Then a pounding on the door woke her. At first, she thought it was the storm. Then she realized someone was actually knocking—loudly!

Amy pulled herself together and stumbled to the door. Who would be out in this storm?

It was Charlie.

She almost collapsed with relief.

"Been worried about yer," he said, shaking himself dry like a dog. "They found flotsam on the beach near town and … "

He stopped, seeing the man in Amy's bed. His face got red and he turned to go. "Sorry!"

"No!" she objected.

Amy laid a hand on his arm and he stopped. She told him about the shipwreck and that she had rescued the drowning sailor from the sea.

Charlie's jaw dropped in disbelief.

"Yer?" he said. "Yer saved him?"

"With a little help from your life preserver," she said. She looked over at the man who was sleeping restlessly.

"I don't know who he is. He hasn't really talked or become very conscious," she said. "He's hurt, or ill, or both, and I don't know what to do for him. Can you get help?"

Charlie went over to the man and peered closely. Felt for injuries.

"Looks like he's got a nasty bump on his head," he said. He checked the sailor all over, making sure he was modestly covered at all times.

"Don't think he's got any broken bones. But he's surely got the fever," he added.

He did not mention that the sailor was naked, though obviously he noticed. After all, desperate times call for desperate measures.

Charlie wrapped his oilskin around him and went to the door.

"I'll fetch help," he said. And with that, he plunged into the storm.

Hours later, Charlie returned. It was late afternoon.

"Ship that wrecked was the *Mollie Kathleen*," he said. "One other man made it to shore at Port Smythe. He's alive but's got some broke bones. He hit the rocks, too. The undertaker will come in the morning and fetch yer man."

"Undertaker?" Amy said, surprised. "He's not dead, Charlie!"

"No, but it's the only wagon in town big enough for a man layin' down and it's covered from the rain," he replied. "Can yer keep him here one more night?"

Amy hesitantly said she could, and thankfully Charlie insisted on staying with them. He'd sleep on the floor, he said. Amy was relieved. What if the man died tonight? She'd not like to be in the cottage alone with a corpse.

She heated some of the leftover stew and Charlie allowed that she had gotten to be a better cook.

"Not as good as me Bess, mind ye, but better'n yer was afore," he complimented her.

They took turns tending the feverish sailor and Charlie suggested she give him some of the willow bark tea Bess had sent her a month or so ago.

"Good fer fevers," he said.

Amy wrapped herself in Rebecca's quilt again after she made a pallet in front of the fire for Charlie. Matilda, for some strange reason, had taken to sleeping at the sailor's feet.

At one point, as Charlie bathed the man's fevered torso, the sailor muttered something to Charlie. The old man looked over at Amy, who tensed.

"Yer need to look away while I help him relieve hisself," Charlie said. Amy did as she was told. She was too tired to keep her eyes open, anyway.

Amy was glad to see morning and that the storm had abated. It still rained lightly.

Before noon, the undertaker's wagon arrived and it took four men to load the sailor into the back. He was taller and larger than any of them. They dressed him in the rags of his now-dried clothes and wrapped him in a blanket before they loaded him into the hearse.

Amy felt sad to see him go, for some reason. But also relieved that she had not had to face her night of abandon with a stranger. It would be her little secret.

CHAPTER FOUR

By Christmas, she knew she was pregnant. She'd been through this before and recognized the signs. At first, she was dismayed and in denial, but she also harbored a secret small joy at the thought. She had been so lonely, and had missed her Rebecca beyond measure. No one here really knew her, and she would not shame her parents by going home. Amy dreaded telling them, but when they came to visit at Christmas, she finally did.

When they first arrived right before the holiday, bearing a tiny Christmas tree and several gifts, they asked her how she was faring. At first, she just said she was fine, but her mother kept eyeing her oddly and finally Amy sat them down and told them.

"I am expecting a child," she said. "Probably next July."

They were beyond stunned.

"But how could this happen?" her mother asked. "You're out here all alone and … oh, it isn't that Charlie creature, is it? Did he take advantage of you? Oh, my, we have to report this to that Lieutenant Stark! And you must come home with us right now!"

Her father put his hand on his wife's arm.

"Let Amy talk," he said, more calmly than his trembling hands revealed.

"It's certainly not Charlie," she told them. Amy said that she could not explain to them what happened, but that no one had forced her and that she was actually happy about the baby.

"Well, can you tell us who the father is? He needs to be responsible for this, do the right thing," her mother insisted.

"He's gone," Amy said. "He won't be back."

She refused to return to her parents' home.

"I am happy here now," she said. "And I won't embarrass you in front of your friends."

"Charlie and Bess take good care of me," she insisted. "I'll let you know when my time comes."

They drove her into town that evening, to the Harbor Inn where they were staying, and treated her to a fine Christmas dinner. After the meal, her mother went up to bed and her father drove Amy home. For December, it was a mild night and the stars were brilliant.

When they got there, they walked over to the sea wall and sat, facing the ocean's cold but restrained waves. The moonlight glinted off his daughter's dark hair, done by her mother into a sophisticated chignon for their evening out.

They didn't talk for a long time. Finally, her father took her hand and asked if there was anything she needed.

"No, I'm fine, really," she said. "I have missed Rebecca so much, I can't regret this baby, even under the circumstances."

He nodded, then changed the subject.

"I heard about the shipwreck," he said. "I heard you saved a man's life. Is that possible?"

Amy told her father about teaching herself to swim, about

seeing the ship hit by lightning, and about saving the sailor. She did not tell him the rest, of course, but he looked at her closely enough to make her blush. Luckily, the dark masked that.

"Keep us informed as to your progress, and think about coming to stay with us when your time is near," he urged. "It won't embarrass us. I'm sure your mother will come up with a suitable story to tell her friends."

"I will let you know," she promised. Then they walked back to the carriage and he kissed her on both cheeks before leaving. They left the next morning, stopping briefly to say good-bye and check on her one last time.

Well, that went better than she expected, she thought. Now, to tell Charlie and Bess.

That afternoon, the Jenkins came to the cottage with a belated Christmas pudding and a new patchwork quilt Bess had been making for her.

Amy invited them in and made tea to go with the pudding. After they ate, the conversation suddenly came to a halt. Amy took the plunge.

"I'm with child," she told them. "I'm sorry if this changes things between us."

Bess looked shocked and Charlie threw a glance at her bed but didn't say anything.

After processing the announcement, Bess asked if the father was going to do right by her.

"He doesn't know, and he never will," Amy replied. "It was … an unexpected encounter and he's gone."

"It better not be that Lieutenant Stark!" Bess declared. "I know he's a widower, but he's got no right to be seducing young women."

Amy almost laughed at the thought. Stark had been here several times, always seemed to approve of her work, but was a man of few words. She could not imagine having a liaison with him. He'd probably wear his uniform to bed.

"He's already got five children; he doesn't need any more," Bess confided. Obviously, the Jenkins knew Stark much better than she did, Amy thought.

IT TURNED OUT TO BE a stormy winter, and Amy was kept busy tending the lighthouse. She also tended the little light growing within her. She ate well, slept better than she had in a long time, and went for long walks on the beach when the weather allowed. She no longer wished an errant wave would wash her out to sea and end her sorrow. A blossom of joy was budding inside her.

One bright winter day, when Charlie came with his wheelbarrow full of rations, she told him she was deathly sick of salted and dried meat.

"You don't need to bring me that much, because I can barely look at another bit of it," she said.

The she asked: "Charlie, do you fish?"

He nodded, and immediately took the hint.

Next time he came, he brought a cane pole, some fishing line and hooks. On a mild February morning, he took her down to the beach and showed her how to use them. She tried several times before she caught one. It was small, but enough for her dinner. Amy was thrilled. Charlie showed her how to clean it. At first, she squirmed at the sight of the slimy guts, but Charlie chided her: "Did yer think they was empty inside?"

And it turned out that Matilda was crazy for fish guts.

Amy thought the fish was delectable, too, even prepared

with her novice cooking skills. After that, she supplemented her diet with fresh fish, and even caught enough to send some home with Charlie a few times. She felt proud to be able to reciprocate their many kindnesses.

As winter wore on, her belly grew. Before it got too big, she decided to go into town to buy fabric for a layette. On a breezy March morning, she wrapped her warmest shawl around her head and shoulders and headed for Port Smythe. The shawl also would hide her emerging pregnancy, starting to show at five months.

The brisk walk to town felt good. When she entered the general store, Mr. Horton greeted her cordially, asking for her list. She handed it to him and began to browse the domestic goods. She found some soft flannel and some yarn she thought might do for her purposes.

At one point she turned around and ran right into Mrs. Agatha Bean. What, did the woman live here?

"And how is the lady of the lamp?" Mrs. Bean asked.

"Fine, thank you," Amy responded, and tried to slide past the older woman—who didn't budge.

"I heard you rescued a sailor from that ship that wrecked," Mrs. Bean said, somewhat skeptically. "In fact, I heard it was the ship's captain. Seems odd a sailor can't swim, don't you think? And who would think a slender young thing like you could rescue anyone?"

Amy felt her anger rise.

"Well, as a matter of fact, madam, I did exactly that. And no one can be expected to swim after a blow to the head," Amy said.

Then her curiosity kicked in.

"How do you know it was the captain? Who told you?"

Amy asked.

Mrs. Bean looked pleased to know something Amy didn't.

"Well," she said, "It was all over town. It was a Captain Fitzgerald. Irish, I hear. He has a funny first name, like Cory or Morry or something. Anyway, he's gone."

Amy felt a cold knot form in her stomach.

"Gone?" she asked, fearful of the answer.

"Back to Ireland, I hear," Mrs. Bean said. She looked hard at Amy.

"After you rescued him, he didn't even tell you his name?" she asked.

"He never really regained consciousness," Amy said, relieved to hear the captain was not dead.

At that point, Mr. Horton had returned to the counter with her short list of items, to which she added the flannel and yarn. Mrs. Bean hovered behind her.

"Doing some sewing and knitting, dear?" she queried.

"Yes," Amy replied, shortly. "Nights get long when you sit alone in a lighthouse."

With that, she gathered her bundle of goods and left the store at a brisk walk toward home. She decided then and there that she could no longer venture into town. The Mrs. Beans of the world were just too nosy!

DAYS LATER, after a light overnight snow, Amy was just washing up her lunch dishes when she heard hoof-beats coming down the lighthouse road. She dried her hands on a towel and went to the door to see who it was.

Her heart sank when she saw it was the Reverend Snead. The last two times he visited, she had hidden quietly, waiting for him to go away. This time, she was caught with the door open to air the cottage and let in the sunshine. It was too late to pretend she wasn't there. She put on the most sincere smile she could manage and left her apron on, to hide her condition a bit. She held her towel in front of her for good measure.

"Good afternoon, mistress," he greeted her as he stepped down from his vehicle and handed her his hat. "Am I too late for lunch? Too early for tea?"

He laughed. She did not. But she invited him in, assuring him she could make him a cup of tea.

"What brings you out here on this snowy day?" she inquired.

He looked at her, as if considering his response.

"Well, I have heard these wild stories around town, some nonsense about you rescuing the sea captain from the *Mollie Kathleen*."

Again, Amy felt anger flare at the general disbelief that a mere woman could do such a thing. So she told him the story, leaving out certain parts, of course.

"You can swim?" he asked, astonished. "How did you learn that?"

"I taught myself," Amy said, with some pride in her voice.

"Well, it's not a very womanly achievement," he replied.

"And just what would have happened to that poor man if I had not been able to swim?" she asked.

The minister was silent for a moment, then said: "Well, I hope you will give up the practice once you are married again."

"I don't plan to marry again," she responded.

Again, he was silent. But not for long.

"Perhaps you just need the right man," he said, "Someone who can control your contrary ways."

Contrary ways?

Who did he think he was?

"Excuse me, but I have to tend the lamp before it gets dark," she said, though dusk was still hours away. "Perhaps you should go now."

Snead looked surprised to be dismissed, but he picked up his hat and gloves and left the cottage, whipping up his horse into a brisk trot down the snowy road back to town.

Amy was somewhat shaken by the encounter, once again dismissing him as a prig and an arrogant ass.

She was still puzzled as to why he had come to call.

Amy was too busy with her work to worry about anything outside her cottage and the lighthouse. She enjoyed living in her own little world for now, growing her baby, being taken care of by people she had come to love, and looking for signs of spring.

The sea roses were beginning to bud and the storms had become less violent. Matilda disappeared one night and didn't show up for dinner. Amy was worried and went looking for her the next morning. She found her in the base of the lighthouse, tucked back in a corner—with a new litter of kittens.

How on earth? Way out here?

Then Amy had to smile at the irony of it.

"Well, old girl, you beat me to it," she laughed, and helped the new mother cat get more comfortable, adding some rags for cat bedding and bringing her a bowl of water and some leftover fish from dinner the night before.

Charlie and Bess made sure Amy had all she needed, too, bringing supplies from town when she asked. True to her word, she had not gone into Port Smythe since the encounter with the nosy Mrs. Bean.

In May, for her birthday, her parents visited once again.

They brought with them Rebecca's cradle, which made Amy's heart lurch with longing. She rubbed her hand over the smooth golden oak and remembered her little daughter. They also brought a trunk full of Rebecca's baby clothes, but Amy could not bring herself to pick them up. It broke her heart; each item of clothing held a memory.

"I understand," said her mother, closing the trunk and motioning for her husband to return it to their carriage. "We'll bring new things for the baby when it's born."

They brought another gift. Her father had brought her a copy of Mr. Melville's *Moby-Dick*. Amy had always wanted to read it—it was published when she was too young to read or appreciate it—and it would help pass the evenings that were now staying light later.

Her pregnancy was extremely obvious by early June. So it was with some dread that she heard a carriage coming up the lighthouse road one afternoon. Yes, it was the pesky Reverend Snead. Again. As he pulled up, Amy rose awkwardly to her feet. There was no hiding her pregnancy now. Time to face the music.

"Good day, mistress," he started to greet her, then almost fell as he stepped down from his surrey. His mouth dropped open and he was, for once, truly speechless.

As usual, it didn't last long.

"You whore!" he shouted. "How . . . how . . . how could you do this to me?"

Before she could respond, he ranted on.

"What adulterous mischief have you been up to? Who did this? Why didn't I know?"

Amy finally got a word in.

"I didn't think it was any of your business," she said, evenly.

"None of my business?" he shouted. "I almost made a fool of myself. I was going to offer you the honor of becoming my wife!"

"But you didn't, and if you had, I would not have accepted," Amy responded. "I'd rather be with child and unmarried than married to a righteous prig."

His face grew red and puffed up like a blowfish. He sputtered. Amy thought he might have what her father called "an apoplectic fit."

Snead charged at Amy and pinned her against the cottage's stone wall.

"You whore!" he repeated. "And here I was being all polite and respectful of your widowhood. You're nothing but a slut! I could have you right now and no one would know or care."

He tried to kiss her, but she turned her head away and his slick lips slid off her cheek. Then she remembered a trick one of her classmates had told her about in school. She raised her knee sharply and, despite her distended belly, kneed him firmly in the crotch. She was as tall as he and her knee found its mark.

Snead doubled over, grasping at himself, and swearing.

"Such words for a minister!" she admonished, then whirled around and retreated into the cottage, locking the door.

After a few minutes, she heard him leave, still cursing.

"Well," she told Matilda, who was taking a break from her kittens to nap in the rocking chair. "The cat's certainly out of the bag now."

Amy waited for the mob of citizens with torches and pitchforks to descend upon the lighthouse, but no one came.

For a week, anyway. Then one day, she heard a horse outside the cottage and went to the door to find Lieutenant Stark.

His face was grim.

"Mrs. Pritchard," he acknowledged and removed his hat. "What's this I hear?"

Amy lifted her chin and walked out to meet him with as much dignity as she could muster.

"Obviously, I am with child," she said. "Does that mean I'm without employment?"

He pondered a few minutes.

"Are you still able to tend the lighthouse?" he asked, bluntly.

"Look for yourself," she offered. He did. He examined every corner, every clean window, checked the level of fuel in the lamp, and looked at her.

"Ship-shape," he declared. "Who's helping you?"

Amy bristled.

"No one, sir," she said. "I do it all myself. I'm very strong."

"And who will help you after the child comes?" he asked. "You will need some help then, at least for a while."

Amy replied that Charlie and his grandson, Jeremiah, would help out in the interim.

"We've got it all figured out," she said.

They were silent a moment. She waited while he pondered.

"So do I still have my post?" Amy finally asked.

Stark gave her a hard look.

"If I hear one report that the lighthouse is not being tended properly, you will have to leave," he said. "Meanwhile, we still don't have enough men to fill the post. But as soon as we do, you will need to find other employment. Unless, of course, you plan to marry. Then your husband can man the lighthouse, if he so wishes."

"I don't plan to marry," Amy replied, somewhat miffed.

"I'd like to stay as long as you'll let me."

Stark grunted, then mounted his horse and left.

She took that as a yes.

But her visitors were not finished.

Two days later, Amy saw a pony cart coming up the track and with dismay realized it was Mrs. Agatha Bean. She almost ran and hid, but decided that her encounters with the Reverend and the Lieutenant had made her tough enough to face anyone.

Mrs. Bean halted her pony and climbed down from the cart. She stood for a moment, hands on hips, looked around and then at Amy.

"Well, you've done it now, my girl," she said. "How on earth did this happen?"

Obviously, the Reverend Snead could not keep a secret.

"It's really none of your business, Mrs. Bean," she said, politely but boldly. "If you've come to lecture me, you can leave right now."

Mrs. Bean held up a hand.

"Oh, the Reverend is in a fine snit," she said. "He's told everyone, of course, even preaching about it from the pulpit. Fornication seems to be his favorite word these days."

The older woman again placed her hands on her substantial hips and chuckled.

"You know, he rejected all the local girls, had his eye on you. One was too plump, took after her mother. One was unable to read the Bible. Another was from a poor family. He knew your father was a banker and thought he'd struck gold. I guess you showed him!"

Amy was dumbfounded. The formidable Mrs. Bean seemed to be on her side.

"Can I offer you some tea?" she asked, chastened by her apparent misjudgment of the woman.

"Always up for tea," Mrs. Bean said. "But first, I have some things for you."

She turned to the pony cart and lifted out a large basket. Then she followed Amy into the cottage.

She set the basket on the kitchen table and opened it. Inside were knitted, crocheted and sewn baby things. Sweet things. Tiny things. Gowns, caps, booties, blankets.

Amy was again stunned. She felt tears begin to threaten.

"Where did you get all this? Why?" she asked.

Mrs. Bean got slightly pink in the face and said: "I shamed the Women's Sewing Circle into it. Told them it was their Christian duty to help a fallen woman. And besides, none of us are very fond of the Reverend. He's a prig."

Amy almost laughed out loud. That's exactly what she thought—and what she had actually called him.

"Oh, Mrs. Bean," she said, "How can I ever thank you?"

"Just take care of yourself and that baby," she replied, not unkindly. Then she became brisk again. "Now I'll take my tea."

After a surprisingly pleasant visit, Mrs. Bean drove off in her pony cart.

"Send word when the baby comes," she called over her shoulder as she departed. "I can bring more."

Amy went back inside the cottage. She walked over to Rebecca's cradle. She looked at the basket of baby clothes and at the half-finished baby quilt she had been sewing. Now, she had all she needed to welcome a new little one into the world.

As July loomed, Amy found it difficult and cumbersome to mount the lighthouse stairs, but figured she had made a commitment to the job and would see it through. Besides, who else would do it? She felt remarkably good, if awkward.

One morning, as she descended the stairs, however, she tripped and fell down the last few steps. She fell heavily, twisting to protect the baby, and landed on her back. She lay there, out of breath, and waited for the stunned feeling to subside.

Just when she was about to get up, her insides were wrenched with a terrible pain. It shot through her like a knife, and made her cry aloud with it. The fall had started her labor and she was alone inside a lighthouse with no help at hand. She wasn't due for a couple of weeks, when her mother planned to be here.

Amy lay in agony for some hours. Every time she tried to rise from the floor, the pain worsened and made her weak and faint. She wondered if she could deliver her own baby, if it came to that. The pains began to get closer together and Amy became desperate to get inside the cottage. She tried crawling, but that only intensified her discomfort.

"Miz Amy?" she heard outside. It was Charlie, come to her rescue once more.

"Charlie!" she cried. And like magic, he appeared at the door. "Oh, miss, what happened t'yer?"

Amy told him she had fallen and could not get herself to the cottage.

"I don't think I broke anything, but I'm afraid I may have hurt the baby," she said, near tears.

"Let's get yer into the cottage, then I'll fetch Bess," he said. "She's done this afore."

It took some effort and it brought Amy a flashback to the night she had rescued the sailor, but Charlie finally got her to her bed in the cottage.

"Hang on," he urged. "I'll be back in the shake of a lamb's tail."

He was as good as his word. He abandoned his wheelbarrow full of provisions and must have run all the way back to his own home, fetched Bess and driven her to Amy's cottage in the pony cart in record time. The pony was huffing when they arrived, not used to being urged to such a pace. Charlie fetched it water while Bess went inside and tended to Amy.

"It's coming fast now," Bess said, after checking Amy's progress. She bustled around the cottage preparing to deliver the baby.

She was right. Things proceeded quickly from this point.

The delivery itself was easier than Amy's first birth experience with Rebecca, but this time her newborn was a boy.

"A fine wee son you have," Bess told Amy, laying the child in his mother's arms.

Afterward she suddenly chilled and began to shake hard for a few minutes, till Bess could warm her with extra blankets.

"Happens sometimes with the second child," Bess said. "Don't know why."

It reminded Amy once again of the night she had rescued the sailor—her baby's father. As the baby's head began to fully dry, she could see he was indeed his father's son—with hair the color of burnished copper.

"Do you have a name?" Bess inquired.

"Yes," Amy replied. "James. After my father. But I think I'll call him Jamie."

CHAPTER FIVE

Rory Fitzgerald emerged slowly, groggily from sleep. The night's thunderstorm was passing over the Irish coast, faint flashes of lightning and low rumblings of thunder fading into the distance. The storm had unleashed his wild dreams once again—dreams that had plagued him since the night the *Mollie Kathleen* had gone down and he had almost died.

He dreamed vividly of the ship sinking like a stone beneath him, the bales of cotton in the hold becoming sodden anchors once the ship was breached by lightning. He dreamed of hitting his head on something hard and thinking he was drowning. He remembered swimming toward the light onshore.

And then, in his dream, he was rescued by a mermaid. She rose up out of the water, put a life preserver around his neck, and towed him to shore. In his dream, her long mermaid's tail magically became human legs as she emerged from the sea. It was a wonder.

The beach seemed like it was miles long and they walked forever before reaching some stone steps. Each step in the wet sand was a struggle. Things kept going black and he feared if he fainted, he would die. But the mermaid/girl would not let him stop.

The sharp rain felt like someone was throwing stones at his skin, and his head hurt as if it were trapped in a vise. The dream was vivid in some ways, murky in others. He lay there in his warm bed, trying to piece it all together.

The strange dream incited flashes of memory. He remembered being so cold that he was afraid his bones would shatter like icicles.

He vaguely recalled being in a bed, shivering, with someone removing his clothes and rolling him around to change the sheets. He could feel again the blissful warmth as the mermaid/girl climbed into bed with him, bringing blessed, life-saving heat.

He most vividly remembered making love to her, and her sweet response. Then things got really vague. He thought someone spooned warm tea down his throat. He recalled in snatches another character—a leprechaun, perhaps?

The last thing he remembered was being loaded into a hearse, thinking that he must have died.

Next thing he knew, he woke up in a hospital. From here, his memory was clearer.

"Where am I? What happened," he had asked a passing nurse, who rushed to get a doctor when she realized he was awake.

"You were in a shipwreck," the doctor told him, while shining a light into his eyes. It hurt. "Actually, I'm told you were rescued by a lightkeeper. A woman, no less. She must have been very brave, and quite strong. "

But what about the mermaid girl? He wondered. Had she ever really existed? He didn't want to ask out loud, it sounded so ridiculous.

"You've had a brain injury," the doctor told him. "It could

take a long time to heal, and you may never feel quite right again. Or it may heal completely. Hard to know these things."

He also had pneumonia, which had left him very weak, but that seemed to be clearing up, the doctor added. Still, he must be quiet for a long time.

One day, his Uncle Seamus came to the hospital and told him his mother was requesting that he be sent back to Ireland to recover from his injuries. Too weak from the pneumonia and head trauma, Rory did not resist.

Two weeks later, he was out of the hospital and aboard the *Shamrock Queen*, headed for home. On the voyage, he experienced something that had never happened to him before: He was seasick. Violently so.

Never was he so glad to see the green hills of Ireland as when the *Queen* docked and his mother and grandfather fetched him. His father had died some years ago from a tropical fever he picked up while sailing in the Caribbean, and these two people had been the mainstay of his life.

Rory spent the next few months recovering. It took him quite a while to overcome the head injury, reluctantly using a cane for a while to stabilize his balance. Finally, he was able to walk unassisted and went for long strolls to restore his physical strength.

Eventually, he was able to ride a horse again without feeling like he was falling off. But it was a painfully slow, frustrating process.

His body began to heal, but the dream persisted. He relived the shipwreck many nights, and always ended with making love to the mermaid girl. Was she real? Had that really happened?

It felt like a piece of his life was missing, unresolved.

On this day, he rose from his bed—luxurious, like the rest of his grandfather's estate house. He washed, dressed and combed his unruly russet hair, then went down to breakfast.

When he entered the dining room, his grandfather was reading the paper and sipping what was probably his fourth or fifth cup of tea. His mother was carefully piling marmalade onto a dainty round of toast. She had a sweet tooth.

They both looked up as he entered. Before they could greet him, he spoke.

"I need to go back to America," Rory announced. "I need to get back to work. And I have some unfinished business."

Rory Fitzgerald was the only grandson of Ronan Fitzgerald, who had started life as a sailor and ended up owning his own company, Shamrock Shipping. Rory's father, Jamon "Jimmy" Fitzgerald, had captained one of his father's ships and favored the Caribbean route because he loved the balmy island weather.

And that's where a tropical fever ended his life.

After his father's death, Rory's mother, Mollie Kathleen, had helped his grandfather with the business. She was educated and helped run the offices. And she raised her son with a heavy helping of business acumen as well as letting him pursue his love of the sea.

She wanted him educated in America, so he could become part of the culture and eventually run the Boston office with his uncle, Seamus O'Brien. Seamus was Mollie's brother and a trusted employee of the Fitzgerald family. They occupied the Fitzgerald home in Boston and took care of things there when Rory was at sea.

Now Rory had been gone from America for a year and a

half since his near-death experience.

"It's time I got back and helped Uncle Seamus with the business," he told his maternal grandfather, Rpnan Fitzgerald, who agreed it was time for him to return to Boston and resume his duties.

"Seamus is getting up there in years and I think he would like to hand off more responsibility," his grandfather said. "And it may be a while before you're fit to sail again."

Rory, despite remembering his seasickness on the trip back to Ireland, agreed readily. He was already dreading the return trip just as a passenger. It was nearly as awful as he imagined. He tried to hide it from the crew, but he was queasy the entire trip back to America. He lost some of the weight he had gained back during his convalescence. Still, he walked the deck every day to stay strong and continue getting control over his balance.

He was relieved to see Boston Harbor, though.

Uncle Seamus met him and took him straight home so his Aunt Bridget, Seamus' wife, could see for herself that her favorite nephew was once again well. After a light supper, Rory wandered out into the garden of his lovely Boston home and sat on a bench. The smell of roses from the garden brought back a faint memory. Where had he last smelled wild roses? For some reason, the scent triggered a renewed sense of urgency to go find the lady lightkeeper who had saved his life.

First, though, Rory had to let Uncle Seamus show him all that had transpired at the office while he was gone. It took several weeks to go over everything. Finally, in July, Rory said, "Stop."

"What?" Seamus asked. "What's wrong with you, boy?

You're so distracted I'm not sure how much of this you're taking in."

"There's something I have to do," Rory replied. "I owe a debt. I have to find the lightkeeper who saved my life and thank her. And I feel like I need to do it now. It's been too long already."

Seamus shook his head.

"A woman, by all accounts," he said. "Imagine that."

Two days later, Rory set out on his horse, a glossy bay gelding named Titan, for Port Smythe. It was a glorious late July day and he enjoyed the journey, which took two long days. When he arrived in town, he took a room at the Harbor Inn and next morning made straight for the lighthouse, which he could see from town. This last mile of his journey seemed to take forever.

As he rode up to the lighthouse and dismounted, the door to the cottage opened. A woman stepped out. She was dressed in simple fashion—a blue cotton skirt and blouse with an apron over all. But her elegant, lovely features and long silken braid stopped him cold.

Suddenly, he found himself speechless.

So, apparently, did the woman.

When he removed his hat, the light breeze ruffled his hair. Her eyes widened when she saw his hair. He saw that she knew immediately who he was. She paled, and looked a little panicked.

Finally, Rory found his tongue.

"Good afternoon, mistress," he began, somewhat formally. "My name is Rory Fitzgerald and I ...."

"I know who you are," the woman said, nervously. She glanced back into the dark door of the cottage, as if afraid. As if she might run inside and bar the door. What had he done to frighten her so?

"I have long been incapacitated by my experience here at Point Peril," Rory tried again. "I am long overdue to give you thanks for saving my life."

The lightkeeper looked at him, as if trying to judge if this was the only reason he had come.

Then a child's voice came from the doorway.

"Mama?" said the child, who was obviously just beginning to walk. He toddled a few steps, then grabbed his mother's skirt and peeked around to look at the stranger. His coppery hair caught the afternoon sun.

Rory's knees almost buckled. No wonder she had reacted the way she did. He recognized that hair. He saw it in the mirror when he combed his own every morning.

His eyes met the mother's and he whispered, "Mine?"

The lightkeeper recoiled.

"Not yours. Mine," she said, and possessively gathered the child up into her arms, holding him close. "Mine. And only mine."

CHAPTER SIX

In the days following Jamie's birth the year before, Amy had barely been able to contain her joy. She was almost unaware of Charlie and his 18-year-old grandson, Jeremiah, taking care of the lighthouse duties. She was barely aware of Bess cooking meals for them. She was completely absorbed in her newborn.

Her parents came and stayed again at the Harbor Inn, bringing gifts and visiting every day, completely captivated by their new grandson. Her father, James, had beamed when she told him the child's name and her mother fussed over them both. She took to brushing Amy's unbound hair again, as she had during Amy's childhood and again when Amy was grieving the loss of her first child, Rebecca.

"Come live with us again," she urged Amy. And Amy had to admit she was tempted. She could use help with the baby. Between her lighthouse duties and Jamie's feeding schedule, she wasn't getting much sleep. She caught naps when she could.

But part of her also treasured the independence she had achieved as a lightkeeper.

"What would your friends and neighbors think?" she

asked, not wanting to subject her parents to the inevitable gossip of an unmarried and long-widowed daughter moving home with a baby. Her mother had no ready reply.

"I'm happy here," she told them. "I want to stay."

When she regained her strength, she started resuming more of the lightkeeper's duties, but had to admit she was glad of Jeremiah's almost daily visits to help. She paid him something out of her small salary and he was grateful for it. On the brink of adulthood, she knew that he, too, was looking to become independent from his parents. When he wasn't at the lighthouse, he was helping out at the blacksmith's shop in the village, but he much preferred being outdoors by the sea to toiling in a smoky, smelly shop.

One day, Charlie showed up with an odd contraption. He called it a "baby pen" and it was like a crib that would sit on the floor, but with tall sides. The bars would keep Jamie safely contained when Amy had to be in the lighthouse. When the baby started crawling, then walking, it would be too dangerous for him to be left unattended and unrestrained.

Amy was amazed at Charlie's ingenuity and grateful for the pen, which resolved a nagging worry that she had been having about that very situation. She made a soft pad for the bottom of the pen and sometimes put him there to nap, since he was rapidly outgrowing the cradle.

She began to settle into her new role.

Jamie celebrated his first birthday in July, with her parents, Charlie, Bess and Jeremiah in attendance. He was a happy and robust child who walked at eleven months and was beginning to chatter. He could say 'mama" and "'orsey"—he loved horses, was fascinated by them. He also could say "no," of course, but would only nod his head vigorously when he meant "yes." He was so curious and fearless, Amy had to keep an eye on him every minute.

One morning as he played on the floor of the cottage with the wooden horse that Charlie carved for him for his first birthday, she heard a rider coming up the road from town. Curious, she stepped outside.

The rider looked a bit familiar, but Amy was sure it was no one she knew. Until he stepped down from his mount and removed his hat. That hair! She knew that hair. She brushed it lovingly every morning and every night—on her son.

A wave of dizziness came over her. She thought she might faint. What was he doing here? She thought she'd never see him again.

He greeted her and started to introduce himself. All she heard was "Captain Fitzgerald."

"I know who you are," she said, more rudely than she intended.

At that moment, Jamie decided to come see the 'orsey, toddled through the doorway and grabbed her skirt, peering around it shyly at the visitor.

The captain stopped speaking, seeming to search for the right words for a long moment. Then his eyes met hers.

"Mine?" he whispered.

"Not yours. Mine," she had said, defiantly, gathering her child up into her arms, holding him close. "Mine. And only mine."

The captain went still and his face flushed.

"I'm sorry," he said gently. "I was surprised to see the little one. I ... I heard you were a widow."

She glared at him, tempted to run back into the cottage and bar the door against this nightmare. She didn't speak.

"We had a bad start," Rory said, taking a deep breath. "I just came to thank you. I have heard repeatedly about the amazing woman lightkeeper who saved my life and I wanted to come back and, well, I assume that person was you. "

Amy didn't respond, except for a slight nod.

He stopped again, staring at Jamie.

"Where's his father?" he asked, bluntly.

"Long gone," Amy replied, feeling like her heart would burst from her chest. "I'm a widow."

"I see," said Rory. There was an uncomfortable pause.

"Well, I just came to thank you, and to see if there was anything you could tell me about that night. It's all muddled in my brain. I had a head injury, you see, and pneumonia. But I keep having these … well … dreams, and flashes of memory. At least I think they're memories. I'm not sure what really happened."

Amy didn't relax. Was this really all he wanted, she wondered?

"Let me put my son down for a nap," she said, "Then we can talk."

He stood there, hat in hand, while she went inside. She shut the door, and leaned against it. Jamie was squirming to get down. "'Orsey, 'orsey," he said, patting the door so she would open it.

"Not now, darling," she said. "It's nap time!"

Jamie did not look pleased. He shook his head.

"No," he said.

"Here's *your* horsey," she said, swooping up the wooden toy Charlie had made. It was the child's favorite plaything. She put Jamie in his pen and gave him the wooden horse, plus a soft blanket. Maybe that would keep him busy, or he would take a nap.

She slipped out the door again, closing it tightly. She took a moment to collect herself, then turned toward the captain.

"I don't' know what I can tell you," she said. "It was pretty frantic and confused. We both almost drowned."

"Please," he said. "Tell me what you remember."

She walked away from the cottage and toward the sea wall. It was her favorite place to think. And she needed to think fast.

As they neared the wall, the scent of the sea roses drifted in the warm morning air. He stopped abruptly, leaned down to smell them, and smiled. That seemed odd to her. She didn't ask him about it because she wanted to get this over with as quickly as possible.

She began by telling him she saw the ship struck by lightning. Then she related what all followed, how Charlie had left a life preserver in the lighthouse and how she used it to retrieve him.

"You can swim?" he asked. He seemed stunned by that.

"I taught myself," she said. "I'm not very good at it, but I can stay afloat and move from place to place."

"Obviously," he said and grinned for the first time. It caught her by surprise. He was very handsome, she had to admit, especially when he smiled.

"Anyway," she continued, "when we got to shore, I managed to get you to help get us both up the steps over there, then we went into the cottage, where you collapsed."

She paused, remembering the tumultuous night. She gave a little shiver at the memory. And she jumped ahead in the narrative.

"The next day, my friend Charlie came and saw your situation, and fetched help. He stayed with us until it came."

He seemed to ponder what she had said—and what she hadn't.

"So I owe this Charlie a debt, too?" he asked.

She hesitated.

"You don't owe anyone a debt," she said, carefully. "It's our job."

"Oh, but I do, and I intend to repay you somehow," he asserted. "I'm here in Port Smythe for a bit to settle the situation of the salvage from the ship and do some other business. May I call on you again tomorrow? I have time while I wait for word from Boston about … business matters."

Amy felt like she was being lied to, but his excuse sounded plausible enough. He seemed very anxious to talk with her some more, and she really did not want to do that.

"I don't go anywhere," she said, relenting. "But I'm always busy, so I don't know how much time I'll have to talk to you. I have a lighthouse to take care of."

"And a little one," he added. "How old is he?"

"He's just over a year," she admitted. "He's big for his age."

"I see," Rory replied. "I am told I was, too."

Amy blushed, but made no response.

From inside the lighthouse, they could faintly hear Jamie calling her. Obviously, he was not taking a nap.

"I'd better go," she said, brushing off her skirt and walking toward the cottage. "Good day, Captain Fitzgerald."

He watched her go, then headed toward his mount.

"And good day to you … um, Mrs. Pritchard, is it? That's what I was told."

"Yes," she replied, and entered the cottage, closing the door firmly behind her.

Inside the cottage, Amy collapsed into a rocking chair

and began to shake. Had she been evasive enough? It wasn't in her nature to lie, and lying always made her so uncomfortable, most people could tell when she was doing it. At least her parents always had.

That afternoon, Charlie showed up, but instead of pushing his usual wheelbarrow full of provisions, he brought the pony cart, and Bess came along, too.

"She's naggin' me to see the baby," Charlie said, without rancor.

Bess climbed down from the cart with his help and hugged Amy. Amy hugged her back, hard. Bess leaned back and looked at the young woman.

"What's wrong, girl?" she asked.

Amy burst into tears, not even knowing she was going to do it.

"What?" Bess asked. "Is it the baby? Is he all right?"

Amy nodded, but continued crying.

"We'd better have a cup of tea and a talk," she said. "Charlie can unload your provisions."

They went inside, where Jamie was finishing his lunch—happily squishing up a plate of cooked vegetables and some crackers. He sat at the little table, on a pillow, with a dish towel tied around him to keep him from falling off or climbing down from the chair.

Amy broke down and told Bess the whole story. Bess was silent until she finished.

"And you fear that the captain, who is the father of this boy, might try to take him away from you? Fiddlesticks! No man in his right mind wants to be saddled with a child on his own," Bess said.

"Really?" Amy said, drying her eyes. "Then why did he

say 'mine' like that and keep asking questions about Jamie?"

Bess snorted.

"Good gracious, girl," she replied, "He can count. And if what you say about their hair is true, it's only natural he'd be suspicious."

Bess seemed to consider the situation for a minute.

"Be honest with him. Maybe he'll help out with a bit of money for the boy," she ventured.

"No!" Amy replied. "I don't want money. I don't want anything from him except for him to go away."

Bess hugged her again before they left—after revealing a basket of sweets she had made for the child—and Amy was sure she'd tell Charlie everything on the way home. Charlie would know his suspicions on the night of the storm were founded, and again she was embarrassed.

But Bess was right, of course. She had to be honest with the man. Just not until she knew a little more about him. Hopefully, when he learned the child was his, he'd head for the hills and never be seen again. Some men were like that. She hoped this one was, too.

The next morning, she heard the clip-clop of horse's hooves come down the path toward the lighthouse. Amy's stomach clenched, but she tidied her hair, smoothing back flyaway wisps into the heavy dark braid, and stepped outside. Jamie was taking his morning nap.

She pointedly ignored his arrival and went straight to the outside pump, where she pumped two buckets of water. It was time to wash the lighthouse windows, she told herself. She lifted the buckets and he stepped forward as if to help her.

"Good morning, Captain," she said. "As you can see, I'm quite busy. No need to help. I have done this many times alone. I'm afraid I don't have time to talk right now."

She headed for the lighthouse and he moved ahead to open the door for her.

"Are you sure I can't help?" he asked. "They look awfully heavy."

She shook her head and mounted the stairs, head high and back straight, a bucket in each hand.

"Maybe you can come back later," she called over her shoulder.

She spent a good half hour cleaning windows but didn't hear him leave. She could see him from her high perch. When she came down, she found him sitting on the sea wall, waiting for her. She sighed.

"That's heavy work for a woman," he said. "Heavy work for anyone. No wonder you're so strong."

She was taken aback by the compliment—well, she considered it a compliment, whether or not he did.

At that point, she heard Jamie calling her from inside the cottage. He had woken from his morning nap. She couldn't keep him penned up forever; he loved the outdoors.

She excused herself and fetched her son from the baby pen, changed his diaper and brought him outside. She set him on a patch of grass between the cottage and the garden with his wooden horse, but he was immediately distracted and drawn to the real horse standing right here in his yard.

"Orsey," he said, with awe in his voice, and stood to toddle toward the bay gelding.

Before Amy could react, Captain Fitzgerald jumped up, picked up the child and carried him to the horse. Amy tried to protest, but the captain assured her the horse was gentle.

He introduced them slowly, and let the child pet its nose.

Titan snorted and Jamie squealed. But he wasn't afraid. He was delighted.

"Have you a carrot?" Rory asked.

Amy nodded and went to the garden, where she pulled a large one. She brushed the dirt off of it and brought it to him. He fed it to the horse while Jamie laughed and clapped his hands as Titan politely took the orange root and munched it down.

Then Rory lifted the boy and set him on the saddle. Jamie was beside himself with delight. The well-trained horse stood quite still, as if he knew precious cargo was on his back.

Finally, Amy asked the captain to take him down. She had nearly panicked when her son sat on the saddle, even though she could tell the captain was being quite careful.

Rory took Jamie down, but continued to hold the boy, and turned to her.

"Please be honest with me," he said. "This child is mine. Am I correct?"

"Yes," Amy responded in a voice barely above a whisper.

They regarded each other for a moment.

"The night of the storm, it was not a dream? I did not make love to a mermaid?" he said, a slight smile twitching at the corner of his mouth. "Thank God that riddle is solved."

Amy was puzzled. Mermaid? She almost smiled herself.

Then she sobered.

"But the child is mine," she said. "You are not responsible for him. I can take care of him myself. You owe me nothing. That night was my mistake. You barely knew what you were doing."

"Well, it seems I did," Rory replied, and he grinned.

Then he also sobered.

"My God," he said. "What hell did I put you through? A widow in that condition, giving birth out here alone, and raising a child by herself?"

"It wasn't hell," Amy said, chin lifting. "It was a joy. Our … intimacy … might have been a mistake, but my son is not. He helped me recover from a deep sorrow. He is the light of my life, my joy, my reason for making a life here."

"The villagers did not shun you for it?" he asked.

"Some did," she admitted, thinking of the Reverend Snead. "But others were kind, and I have Charlie and Bess—my provisioner and his wife. They have been the best of friends to me. Even the town gossip has taken me under her wing."

"And my parents have been completely supportive. They visit as often as they can. They all adore Jamie."

Rory seemed surprised.

"We need to talk a lot more," he said.

He set Jamie down on the grass again, handed him his wooden horse, then turned to Amy.

"When?" he asked. "When can we talk?"

"We can have lunch, after which Jamie will take his afternoon nap," she said, and sighed. "We can talk then."

She picked up Jamie and took him in with her while she prepared something to eat. They ate a light lunch of leftover cold roast mutton and vegetables from her garden. At first, they struggled to make small talk.

Since Amy didn't seem to be forthcoming, he told her about his family—his mother and grandfather in Ireland, the shipping company, and how Shamrock Shipping was building a ship to replace the one lost in the storm.

Again, he thanked her for saving his life.

Amy shrugged.

"Anyone would have done the same," she insisted. He shook his head, as if disagreeing with her, but did not respond to that.

Then Rory asked Amy how she became a lightkeeper. She decided to tell him the unvarnished truth.

"My husband, Reuben, died in the war," she told him. "Then my daughter, Rebecca, died from an illness. I had no one but my parents and a lot of grief to work through. I heard about this job and it sounded perfect for me. A time to heal, away from everyone and everything that reminded me of the family I had lost. And to be independent, to become my own person, for the first time in my life."

She had stopped eating and looked at him, willing him to understand.

"Now you know why Jamie is so precious to me, despite the circumstances."

Rory did not know how to respond. They continued eating in silence for a while.

Then Amy changed the awkward subject and asked him, "How many sailors were lost when your ship went down in the storm?"

"It was a small skeleton crew, making a return trip from the Carolinas," he said. "My first mate, Roscoe, made it ashore in Port Smythe, injured but has since recovered. The other ten drowned. I didn't know them well, because they weren't my regular crew. But any loss of life is a tragedy."

He explained that when the ship went down, he temporarily caught hold of a chunk of wood from the ship that helped him make it toward shore. Then he lost the piece of wood when a large wave dashed him under. And he hit his head as he was dashed into the rocks, perhaps losing consciousness for a few moments.

"I just kept swimming toward the light—your light," he said. "Good thing I did."

He told her that he felt a thick rope and grabbed it.

"That was my hair," she said, gesturing toward her braid. "You pulled me under for a moment. I had a life preserver Charlie had given me and I used that to tow you ashore."

"It's starting to make sense now," Rory said. "It's all been such a muddle in my head."

After lunch, although Jamie was enchanted with the visitor, and fought drowsiness with all his might, he finally did fall asleep on Amy's lap, and she placed him in his baby pen.

The two went outside and once again sat on the sea wall. Both were silent a long time, both seeming to be lost in their respective thoughts.

"I need to do right by you," Rory finally said.

"No," Amy said. "You owe me nothing."

"Well, I probably should marry you and make you an honest woman," he began, not quite smiling.

"No!" Amy responded, and stood up. "I lost one husband already. I'm not about to marry someone I don't even know, and out of obligation besides. Much less a sea captain who, as we both know, can die in the next violent storm. My son does not need that and neither do I."

Rory looked shocked at her intense reaction.

"What can I do for you then?" he said. "Money? Do you need money? I'm sure a lightkeeper's pay isn't all that bountiful."

"I don't need your money, either," she said. "I have all I need here and if I should need more, my parents are always willing to help. Not that I would ask."

He seemed taken aback by her defiant stance, hands on hips, head high.

"Well, then, what can I do?" he asked. "I'm not just going to get on my horse and ride away, as if nothing ever happened."

That's exactly what Amy was hoping he would do. She looked around, seeking some chore for him, and saw the pile of wood waiting to be chopped.

"There!" she said, pointing at the firewood. "You can chop wood for the winter. It's getting too hard for Charlie and, as you said, you owe him something, too."

With that, she stalked back to the cottage.

Rory sat on the sea wall, watching her go. Then he shrugged, walked over to the wood pile, took off his shirt and picked up an axe.

Amy busied herself in the cottage for the next few hours, but after Jamie woke from his nap, he fussed until she let him go outside. She had to go up and check on the fuel for the lamp, anyway, so she did what she usually did. She tied Jamie to the clothesline with a long, soft rope looped and knotted around his waist. He could sit and play and toddle back and forth, but only go so far. She would only be gone a few minutes.

She ignored Rory, chopping wood and sweating in the afternoon sun. Finally, she felt sorry for him and fetched him a mug so he could get a drink out of the outside pump. He thanked her and she ignored him, going into the lighthouse. She was only gone about ten minutes, but when she came back down, Rory was gone. And so was Jamie.

Amy panicked. The untied rope lay on the ground. The horse was still there, though, munching on grass in the shade of the lighthouse. She ran to the sea wall and heard squeals—

Jamie's voice! Then she saw them, out in the water. Too far out.

She ran down the steps and along the sandy beach to where they were. Clothing littered the shoreline.

"What on earth are you doing?" Amy shouted to Rory. He was chest-deep in the ocean, holding Jamie up near his shoulder. They were both laughing.

"We're taking a bath," Rory called to her. "Come join us! I know you can swim."

Amy looked down at her skirt and shoes.

"Not in this," she shouted. "Bring my son here right now."

Rory realized he'd overstepped boundaries, so he started for shore. With each step, the ocean's level dropped till he was only waist-deep. And he kept coming. Amy realized with a start that they were both stark naked. Well, how else would you take a bath?

She quickly turned around and Rory laughed. He emerged from the water behind her and set her son down beside her, on the beach.

"He had a little accident, and I was all sweaty, so we decided to go for a swim," he explained, and she could tell from his voice that he was right behind her. "I didn't mean to frighten you."

Amy bent down and gathered up her naked little boy, wrapped her apron around him and marched back along the beach, up the steps and into the cottage.

She was furious. The man was presumptuous and infuriating. How dare he take her son into the ocean like that, without even asking her?

She didn't know what to do.

For the rest of the week, Rory came every day, chopped wood until she had enough for two winters, and they kept an unspoken truce with each other.

Charlie came one day when Rory was there—seemed like he was always there—and finally met the sea captain. At first, Charlie was bristly toward the sailor until he saw how much little Jamie adored him. And Amy, if not exactly friendly, seemed to tolerate the man. Then Charlie started to warm up to him, too.

Jeremiah came, too, to help Amy with some chores, but found that the captain had already done them. Jeremiah was less friendly than his grandfather.

"You better do right by Miss Amy," Amy overheard the young man threatening Rory one day.

"She heard Rory sigh.

Well, I've offered, but she turned me down cold," he said in reply. Jeremiah looked surprised but said no more. After that, he was grudgingly friendly.

Bess made a surprise inspection on another day and pronounced the captain "a fine specimen of a man," but had her reservations about whether he had taken advantage of her girl during the storm.

"He did not take advantage of me," Amy clarified. "It just happened in the chaos of the night. It was my poor judgment, and he was just being a man."

Bess snorted, but said no more.

One day when Rory arrived, Jamie toddled toward him, arms up, and cried, "Papa!"

Amy glared at Rory.

"Did you teach him that?" she accused.

Rory looked chastened, but smiled as he picked up the boy.

"Maybe," he said. "After all, I am."

Amy had no response.

And then there was another visitor.

Lieutenant Sparks came riding up one day, unannounced as usual, and instead of going directly into the lighthouse, asked to speak to Amy inside the cottage.

She left Jamie outside with Rory, who was repairing part of Titan's bridle, and invited her boss inside.

Sparks got right to the point.

"As of September," he said, "you will need to find other employment, if indeed you intend to do so. Perhaps you will marry?"

He glanced outside, where Rory was giving the boy a ride on his back.

Amy started to protest, but he cut her off.

"I have offered young Jeremiah the lightkeeper's post. He seems quite capable, and he's of age now, I understand. He did not want to take it, out of loyalty to you, but I told him if he did not, you would still be out of a job. He wanted to tell you himself first, but I assured him that was my duty, not his."

At first, Amy was shocked, then she was disappointed. She loved living here, tending the lighthouse and her garden, raising Jamie on her own. She had known it would end someday, but had hoped it would not be so soon.

"I understand," she said, trying not to cry. She looked at him, trying to read his expression.

"But … did I do a good job?" she asked.

"You did an excellent job," he said, "particularly under the circumstances, and I very much regret this decision, but the Lighthouse Service needs young men and Jeremiah is a perfect candidate."

Amy offered him tea but he declined once again. He always did. Then he left.

Rory watched him go and looked questioningly at Amy.

"Are you all right, lass?" he asked.

"Seems I am out of a job," she said, letting it sink in. "I need to be gone by September. That's just a few weeks away. I don't know what to do."

Rory moved to her and put his arms around her. She stiffened. He had not touched her since his return. He kissed the top of her head and she felt a frisson of something alien—pleasure?—rush through her body. It felt good to be comforted by someone at this moment, but she finally pushed away.

"What can I do to help?" he asked.

"I thank you for your concern," she said. "But this is something I have to figure out myself."

With that, she turned and walked down the stone stairs to the beach and he watched as she took off her shoes and began a long walk that would not bring her back for more than an hour. She had entrusted Jamie to his care without any admonitions or threats. Without question.

She trusted him that much, finally.

Amy hardly slept that night, trying to decide what to do. The next morning, when Charlie arrived, she gave him the news. But Jeremiah had already told his grandfather what had happened.

"Bess and me are worried about yer," he admitted. "We knows how much this post means to yer."

"I probably will need to go stay with my parents again till I find something else to do," she said. "Seems like I always have to fall back on them when life kicks me in the teeth."

But Rory arrived late in the morning—much later than

usual—and he had another idea. He had a proposal.

"Come with me to Boston," he said, almost immediately. "I know you are educated, and can do ciphers, and I desperately need someone to help my bookkeeper, Simon, with his work. Simon is still sharp, but losing his eyesight. He needs an assistant, and you would be perfect."

"No," Amy started to reply, but he held up a hand to stop her.

"Please, just listen for once. You say you won't marry me because you don't know me, but you would have time to get to know me, and even if you decide not to do so, I would have a chance to know my son, and for him to know his father. I'm not walking away, no matter what.

"I have not had business in Port Smythe since that very first day I came here, and you probably guessed that. No matter where you go, I will find a way to be near and to be part of his life. And yours. Even if I have to chop countless cords of wood."

Amy was stunned. He had this all figured out. He was planning her life for her. Her first instinct was to protest. But then she considered what he had to say and admitted he might have a point.

"But where would I live?" she asked. "I have little money. Can I afford to live in the city?"

"That's easy," Rory replied. "We have a guest cottage behind the main house in Boston. You can live there till you get on your feet. And the job pays much better than a lightkeeper's salary, I promise you."

He said she would only need to work half days so she could still be with Jamie a good part of the time, and she'd have people to care for him when she was at the office. She would not have to move back in with her parents again and she could become her own woman, earn her own way, remain as independent as she wanted.

Amy was tempted. After he left for the day, she took Jamie to the beach and let him play in the shallow, undulating waves created by the incoming tide. She would miss the sea, but there was no guarantee she could live near it again, anyway.

The lighthouse was hard work and it was getting harder as Jamie got older. How long could she do it, anyway?

She could see the child's attachment to his father was already strong. Should she deny him that relationship? And she was becoming fond of the man herself, because he was so kind to her and he had that contagious laugh, when he was not being infuriating.

The next morning, when Rory arrived, she confronted him.

"Is this a real job, not just one given out of pity?" she asked.

"It is indeed," he replied. "Simon needs help."

"I can live in this guest house by myself—with Jamie, of course—and you won't expect any 'privileges'?" she asked.

"Certainly," he said. "I compromised you once, and it won't happen again. Without your express permission, of course."

She eyed him warily.

"And there are other people in the house, so we will not be living together alone?" she asked.

"My Uncle Seamus and Aunt Bridget live there, too, and a few servants. I'll even get you a nanny to watch the boy when you're not there, someone who meets with your approval. We can't keep tying him to the clothesline, after all."

Amy thought a moment. She took a deep breath, making a decision.

"All right, I'll go," she said. "But if any of these things prove not to be true, I will leave immediately."

"You won't be sorry, lass," he promised, happy with her decision.

She wasn't so sure, but it was the best option before her right now.

Saying good-bye to the lighthouse and her friends was harder than she imagined.

She assured Jeremiah that she was not angry or resentful. She was happy that he seemed thrilled with the new post, and he had long ago made friends with Matilda, who had taken to following him everywhere he went and watching him work, as if supervising. As Charlie had said before, she was "the lighthouse cat" and she was more loyal to the place than to its people.

"She's a good mouser," Amy told Jeremiah, "and she likes to be rocked."

Charlie and Bess were both in tears as they helped her pack her few belongings into the wagon that would follow the carriage Rory brought to fetch her and Jamie.

Charlie kept sniffling, wiping his nose with a hankie, and muttering about getting a cold, but Bess was openly crying.

Amy kept the cradle and the baby pen and all of Jamie's things. She left the bed for Jeremiah, who had no furniture of his own, along with the rocking chair Bess had given her. She did take her own rocker, her writing desk and the carved chest that had been a wedding gift from Reuben.

Tearful good-byes were exchanged and the three of them—Rory, Amy and their son—headed off on the journey to Boston. It would take two full days and they would stop at an inn overnight. She had written to her parents, so they knew where she was going, and asked them to bring some of her better clothes to her new home, and to come meet her new employer, Captain Fitzgerald.

She would explain all when they next met, she promised.

At first, the ride was awkward. Amy was unsure of what she was about to encounter and Rory seemed to be choosing his words carefully so as not to frighten her off. Finally, they found common ground. Books.

"I saw you had a copy of *Moby-Dick* in your cottage," he ventured. "Did you read it?"

"Of course, I read it," she said. "Twice."

"What did you think?" he asked.

She was complimented that he seemed to actually want her opinion.

"It was a wonderful story, but very tragic, I think," she said. "Do sailors all become so obsessed with such things as white whales?"

Rory gave thought to his answer.

"When you're at sea," he said, "the ship becomes your world. There is nothing else but ocean as far as you can see, most days. It could be easy, I think, to develop such an obsession, but Captain Ahab seemed to me to be more prone to it than most."

They discussed the book further, then went on to others.

"I heard a Frenchman named Jules Verne is working on a book about underwater exploration. As if such a thing would be possible," Rory said. "Still, the premise is fascinating. I just don't see how one could be in an underwater ship for very long, though. You'd run out of air."

They discovered they had read many books in common and Rory promised her full access to his library at his home.

When they stopped for the night, she and Jamie shared a room. As she readied herself for bed, she felt the first stirrings of excitement at her new venture. It hadn't seemed real until now.

The second day's journey was slowed by rain, and they didn't arrive at their destination until after dark. Jamie had been restless much of the day, confined to the coach. But Rory had endless patience with him.

As they neared the house, even in the dark, Amy could see the house was very large and very grand. She was a little stunned. She didn't know her wood-chopping sea captain lived so well.

But for now, she was physically and emotionally exhausted. She would get a better look in the morning.

Aunt Bridget welcomed her with open arms—literally. The petite woman embraced Amy as if she were a long-lost daughter, and caressed the face of the sleeping Jamie.

"Oh, he's a lovely boy," she said. She took Amy's hand.

"You'll spend the night in the main house tonight," she said. "We'll get your things moved into the guest house in the morning, if that's all right with you," Aunt Bridget said.

Amy was too tired to protest.

CHAPTER SEVEN

The morning sun streaming through huge, lightly curtained windows woke Amy. It took her a few moments to get her bearings before she remembered where she was. She rolled over and there was a bright head of copper hair on the pillow next to her. She quietly slipped out of the bed, so as not to wake her son, and found a soft robe draped over a chair near her. She put it on. It was a little short, but otherwise fit her.

She went into the bathroom, adjacent to her room. It was a real bathroom, with a sink and claw-foot tub and commode—and it had hot running water! What luxury! She washed and put the robe back on while she sought out her clothes from the night before. They lay neatly folded on another chair. For traveling, she had worn her second-best skirt of navy blue and her second-best shirtwaist and a warm shawl Bess had made and given to her.

"Mama?" Jamie sat up in bed, rubbing his eyes. He looked around, puzzled. She went to him and pulled him onto her lap.

"This is your Papa's home, darling," she said. She took him to the window, which overlooked a garden and a cottage.

"That must be our new house," she said.

Amy looked around the room she was in. It was as large as her whole cottage at the lighthouse. Captain Fitzgerald must be quite well to do, she thought. Well, no wonder he took pity on her. Her small cottage and her menial job must have seemed quite pathetic to him.

Well, she wasn't taking anyone's charity. She would live here only as long as necessary, then get her own lodgings. In the meantime, she would be as gracious as possible about it.

She dressed her son and they left the room, descending a grand staircase to the main level. Once in the front hall, she didn't know which way to go.

"Do you need help?" Rory asked, coming out of a room on the far side of the foyer. It must be his office, she decided.

"Good morning," Amy said, a little stiffly. She wasn't about to let him get the upper hand, even on his own turf. She didn't want him to get any ideas. "I need to find sustenance for Jamie. He says he's hungry."

Rory was puzzled by her terse reply, but put it down to her being disoriented in an unfamiliar setting. He might feel the same in her situation.

"You both must be starving," he said, kindly. "Come this way."

He crossed the front hall and led them to a room on the other side—a dining room. The bright, sunny space had lovely furniture and a sideboard laden with wonderful food. It smelled heavenly; Amy's mouth watered.

"Eat, Mama!" Jamie demanded. Rory directed her to a high chair for the child and she took the place beside it. Rory stood next to her.

"What would you like?" he asked.

"Anything," Amy replied.

So he filled plates for them both—coddled eggs, rashers of bacon, crisp toast with golden butter and ruby-colored jam. He brought a pot of hot tea to the table, and a glass of milk for Jamie. She felt strange, letting him wait on her. It was a novel experience. Amy had never seen her son eat so much at one sitting—and had to admit, neither had she consumed so much at a single meal for years.

Rory watched them, smiling. Suddenly, Amy became self-conscious.

"Aren't you eating?" she asked.

"Already did," he replied. "I decided you two sleepyheads needed your rest, and I was too hungry to wait for you. Sorry."

Realizing that she felt awkward with him watching her eat, he excused himself and went back to his office.

"Come find me when you're finished," he said.

Once replete, they did just that.

Amy led Jamie by the hand across the grand foyer to Rory's office. She stopped, staring at the walls, covered floor to ceiling with books. It also was a library.

"Oh, my," she said. "My father had a lot of books in his office, but nothing like this."

She walked to the bookcases and ran a finger reverently over the titles. Authors like Ralph Waldo Emerson, Henry David Thoreau and Nathaniel Hawthorne were tucked in between books on astronomy, seafaring, shipbuilding and other subjects that might engage a learned man who also spent a lot of time at sea. The room also had a fireplace flanked by two chairs and side tables. It felt quite cozy. But her attention went back to the treasure trove of reading material.

"Feel free to take anything you want to read," he invited

her. "And there's also a good book shop in town where I have an account. You also may make use of that."

Jamie had found a large atlas on the bottom shelf, pulled it out onto the floor and opened it. He stared, fascinated, at the colorful maps and pointed to the pages as if he knew what they were.

"Pretty," he declared.

Rory and Amy both laughed, aloud and together, and it surprised them both. It felt intimate, and scared Amy.

"I guess I'd better see where I'm going to live," Amy said, businesslike, changing the atmosphere in the room.

"Of course," Rory said, rising from his desk. He closed the large leather portfolio he had been studying. He had kept that with him in the coach on their journey and Amy was curious about its contents. She assumed it was probably building plans for his new ship or some such, but before she could ask, they were interrupted.

At that moment, Aunt Bridget bustled into the room.

"Riordan James Fitzgerald," she began. "Where are your manners?"

His middle name was James? Amy didn't know. He'd never said. Riordan? Must be Irish, she thought. Rory fitted him better.

"It's fine," she told his aunt.

'Well, where are my manners, as well?" Aunt Bridget said. "We didn't do formal introductions last night. You and the boy were almost asleep when you arrived.

"I'm Bridget O'Brien, and my husband, who you saw briefly last night, is Seamus O'Brien. Rory's mother's brother. You may call us Aunt and Uncle, as everyone does.

"I can't tell you how welcome you are! I've had the staff

pack your things and move them to the cottage for you. Do you have more things coming?"

"Not really," Amy said, oddly charmed by the woman's no-nonsense, take-charge attitude. "My parents should be here in several weeks with a few more clothes, but that's all there is for now."

"Well, let me show you the guest cottage," Aunt Bridget said. And Amy followed her out of the room, with Rory carrying his son.

They exited through the French doors on the back side of the staircase, walked along a flagstone path through a garden, and to the front door of the cottage. It was charming, looking like a little Irish thatched hut.

"It's small," Aunt Bridget warned, "but quite comfortable."

The guest cottage was much larger than the lighthouse cottage, with a living area, complete with fireplace, a small kitchen area and a separate bedroom with a large closet/dressing room. There also was a fully functioning bathroom. The cottage was quite spacious and fully furnished, much nicer than her former abode.

The baby pen was set up in the dressing room, along with a child's cot. Her trunk was set at the end of the bed and satchel with personal items on the dresser. Her rocking chair and Rueben's chest were in the living room. Rebecca's starburst quilt was still in the trunk. Her most treasured things were here. All of them.

"It's perfect," Amy said, and Aunt Bridget beamed. On impulse, Amy hugged her. "Thank you."

"Now, maybe I should show you around Boston a bit, to get you oriented," Rory finally spoke. "I've ordered a carriage for this morning, if you're up to another carriage ride," he added. "It's a beautiful day for an outing."

It indeed was a lovely fall day and Amy didn't quite know what to do with herself, with no lighthouse duties to perform. So she agreed.

"I'd change my clothes, but I don't really have anything appropriate for a Sunday outing," she said, looking down at her well-worn skirt and shirtwaist.

"What you're wearing is just fine for now, but I can see we'll just have to take you shopping, my girl," Aunt Bridget said. "For now, though, I'll leave you two to get settled."

She looked at Rory.

"*We* will leave you two to get settled," Aunt Bridget repeated, emphatically, looking at mother and son, and Rory reluctantly left with her.

Amy led Jamie around the room, telling him all about their new lodgings, to help him become acquainted. She unpacked his small trunk and found his horsey, which she knew would comfort him in the strange surroundings. She tested her new bed—soft, inviting and larger than any she had ever had.

She had grown up in a nice house. Her father, after all, was a banker. But her parents were not exactly spendthrifts, or self-indulgent people. She always had nice clothes, good shoes, and she never wanted for anything essential. But even this cottage was more luxurious than her childhood home. And the main house was, to be blunt, a mansion.

As far as she could see, the home was surrounded by vast lawns, nicely landscaped, and it sat on a hill above the town. The lawns were lovely, but she preferred the little garden between the house and guest cottage for its charm and for the variety of plants she intended to explore. Maybe they'd let her put in a small vegetable garden, if they didn't have one. But no! She wouldn't be there that long, she told herself. And spring was still far away. Anything could happen between now and then.

She must not get too used to such luxury, she warned herself. These were not things she would be able to afford on her own. And that was her goal, after all. To be on her own. Independent, accountable to no one.

Jamie crawled up onto the bed beside her, his horsey tucked under his arm. He trotted it across her arm, making clip-clop sounds as it galloped from her wrist to her shoulder. Then he had the horsey kiss her, and climbed down from the bed again to explore his own room. Curious, he crawled onto the cot and tried it out, such as she had the bed. He hopped off again and sat on the floor, trotting his wooden horse around the braided rug.

A firm knock at the door announced the arrival of his father.

"Papa!" Jamie cried in anticipation as he ran to the door and tried to open it. Luckily, Amy noticed, the latch was too high for him to reach. She got up and went to the door, opening it.

"Are you ready to see Boston?" Rory asked.

With that, they all went through the house, to the front, and got into a lighter, smaller carriage than the coach that had transported them to the city. The windows were bigger and Jamie could see out of them by standing on the seat. Amy kept a hand firmly clutched in his jacket to keep the boy from losing his balance.

Rory took them down the hill from his home to the Boston Commons, past the Old North Church and other landmarks, giving a refresher course in the Revolutionary War as they went. Everywhere, the trees were turning those glorious New England colors—scarlet, crimson, orange, gold and yellow. After a while, they got out and walked around some of the shops.

Rory took her to his favorite book shop and introduced her to the owner, Samuel Wordsworth. The older man bowed graciously over Amy's hand in an old-world gesture.

"Welcome," he said. "Any friend of Captain Fitzgerald's is a friend of mine. And before you ask, yes, Wordsworth is really my name. And with a name like that, I really had no choice of professions, now did I?"

They all laughed, though it was obvious this was his standard introductory line to newcomers.

"Mrs. Pritchard is new in town, and will be working for the shipping company. Meanwhile, my family is looking after her," Rory explained.

Wordsworth took Rory's directive that she was to select any books she wanted, and that they were to be charged to his account.

Rory was surprised to see Amy stiffen and blush.

As they left the shop, he tried to take her arm and she pulled away.

"How dare you?" she hissed. "Now that man thinks I am your mistress!"

Rory was stunned, then abashed.

"I'm sorry," he said. "I only meant for you to have free access to any books you might want. I will make a point of talking to Mr. Wordsworth so he understands that you are my houseguest, not my mistress."

"Fine," Amy said. "But do you think for one minute he

looked at Jamie and didn't know he was your son?"

She took a deep breath to calm herself.

"I'm not sure this is all going to work."

Rory took her by the shoulders right there on the street.

"I don't care what anyone says, I am not going to deny Jamie—ever," he said. "People will always think what they want. If it bothers you, then you must find a way to come to terms with it."

Amy had never seen him angry like this, and she had to admit that she really didn't care much what people thought, either. As long as it didn't affect her son.

"You're right," she confessed. She waited a beat and shook off the moment. "Now, where do we go next? I'm hungry, and so is Jamie."

Surprised by her quick capitulation, Rory let go of her.

"I apologize for my outburst," he said. "I should have known what it might look like and been more thoughtful of your feelings. Truce?"

She nodded, still somewhat miffed.

"All right, then, I'm hungry, too, and I know just the place to take care of that," he said.

The three of them had lunch in a charming little English pub, then returned home so Jamie could nap.

"Thank you for showing me the city," Amy said.

She looked around the cottage.

"Is there food here? Can I make supper for myself and Jamie?"

Rory laughed.

"Aunt Bridget would not have any of that!" he said. "You'll dine with us—Jamie, too. We're very informal here, so no need to dress for dinner."

"Tomorrow, we'll find a nanny for Jamie and as soon as we've done that, I'll take you to the shipping office to meet my bookkeeper and get started to work."

Amy looked pleased at that, so he left her with the promise to see her at dinner.

Rory left, happy that he had made her happy. For now, anyway.

CHAPTER EIGHT

The next day dawned cloudy but dry. Amy took her son in to breakfast, which he once again devoured. She ate lightly, nervous about what was to come.

At breakfast, Rory told her Aunt Bridget had lined up three women to possibly become nanny to Jamie. She could interview them and see which one she wanted. Amy had never interviewed anyone before. The closest she had come to a job interview was her own, for the lightkeeper's post. What would she ask? Can you carry two buckets of water upstairs? That would hardly do!

"How will I know which one is best?" she asked Rory.

"Follow your instincts," Rory said. "When I hired Roscoe as my first mate on the *Mollie Kathleen*, I hired him not because of what he knew, but because of his willingness to learn. It worked out well. Think about what's most important to you for someone who will be doing your job, taking care of the boy, while you are gone. And Aunt Bridget is usually here, so she'll have someone to ask, if she has questions or a problem."

Amy finally met the three candidates, one at a time, using the cottage kitchen table for an interview setting. The nanny would be working in the cottage, not the mansion, so this was a good way to start, Amy thought.

She asked each one about their experience as a nanny. The first two had some. One was an older woman, stern and with lots of rules. Amy didn't like her. Jamie hid behind his mother during the interview.

The second was middle-aged, laughed too loudly and hugged Jamie roughly, so that he again retreated behind his mother.

The third was a young girl, just nineteen, whose mother had died when she was twelve and who had spent the past seven years raising her five younger siblings. She had a pleasant voice and brought Jamie a tiny stuffed bear she had made herself. Jamie approached her and took the toy, then stood listening to the two women talk. As she talked, the girl, whose name was Susan Beddoes, absentmindedly reached out and ruffled Jamie's hair gently. The child smiled and moved closer to her.

Needless to say, Amy had no tough decision here. As it turned out, Susan was the granddaughter of an acquaintance of Aunt Bridget's. The older woman said she could use Susan for various other duties when not needed as a nanny, and Susan could live in the servant's quarters. If Amy had to guess, they were probably a step up from the girl's current living conditions.

Susan moved in the next day. That afternoon, Rory sent a carriage for Amy after lunch, to take her to the shipping company's offices. They were near the wharf and she could smell the sea air as they arrived. Amy liked that.

The white clapboard building was two stories high and the top floor had a view of the ships in the harbor. Amy liked that, too. She was shown upstairs to Simon Trask's office, across the hall from Rory's own. He came out to greet her and introduce her to Simon.

Trask had a head of unruly white hair and thick glasses, and he stood and sat a little bent—most likely from trying to see the pages on which he was working. He took her hand and welcomed her warmly, showed her to a small desk opposite his own, and held out her chair for her.

"Let me tell you what I do," Trask said. "Then I'll show you the books."

Rory hovered in the doorway.

"Shoo!" Trask said. "I can do this by myself, Cap'n Fitz."

Rory retreated, but left both office doors open. They knew he could hear every word they said.

Simon Trask set about explaining how he did the books, and Amy took notes. Basically, she would go over his work every day and check his figures. Because of his failing eyesight, he sometimes saw a 3 as an 8, or a 7 as a 9. And so on. Once she became familiar with the bookkeeping system, he would train her in how to do the initial work herself, allowing him at some point to retire.

"Retire?" Amy asked. "I thought I was just going to be your second set of eyes, your helper."

"Well, I didn't say I was going to retire tomorrow, now did I?" Trask replied, smiling.

Amy took to the work quickly, finding only a few errors—but important ones. Trask praised her acumen, and she glowed in the light of his approval.

She was surprised when Rory came to the door and told her it was time to go. It was getting dark out! Amy had thought the afternoon would drag on, especially since it was literally her first time she had really been away from her son. But it had flown by.

In the carriage, on the way home, she told him about what she learned that day, how pleased Simon Trask had seemed with her work. She literally chattered. Rory had never seen her like this. It pleased him greatly. He had made a good decision, made her happy. It was progress.

Jamie was thrilled to see her. He hadn't been too happy about his mother leaving him that afternoon, but Susan had quickly distracted him with a game of hide-and-seek. Jamie didn't quite get the concept at first, "hiding" in plain sight, but eventually he did—and he loved it. Now, he wanted to be the person hiding all the time.

"My hide," he told Amy, then crawled under his cot and peeked out at them.

Again, she and Rory laughed at him together. For a moment, they felt like a real family, until Amy reminded herself this was just temporary.

She let Susan go for the day, thanking her, and told Rory she'd see him soon at dinner, then she collapsed onto her bed. Jamie crawled up beside her and snuggled into the crook of her arm.

"Do you like Susan?" Amy asked. Jamie nodded.

"Susan hide," he said. "My hide, too."

Before she knew it, they were both asleep.

When she woke, it was late—much too late for dinner. But she found a warm pot pie on the kitchen table, set for two. A small jug of milk was left for Jamie and a jug of lemonade for her. It would do just fine.

The next morning, at breakfast, Aunt Bridget fussed over them.

"This is too much for you," she said. "He can't work you this hard!"

Amy laughed as loud as she ever had in her life.

"Aunt Bridget, I've been tending a lighthouse for two years. Carrying buckets of water upstairs, washing huge windows, refilling lamp fuel, tending a garden, making my own meals, and finally raising a baby on my own. This is nothing compared with that!"

Aunt Bridget grumbled, but relented.

"Well, if you say so," she said, "but don't let that boy bully you. He has told me what happened, and I don't want you to be fretting about that. Just know we're here to make sure you get the life you want, Seamus and I. We love Rory. He's like a son to us, but he's never been told no. I'm glad you can stand up to him. I think that's why he's so mad about you. I've never seen him like this."

Amy stared at the older woman.

"Mad about me?" Amy said, staring at Aunt Bridget as if she had grown a beard. "He feels responsible for me. I've told him he's not. But he insists on helping me. It's guilt, and his natural generosity. That's all."

Now it was Aunt Bridget's turn to laugh.

"Oh, my girl, but you are blind," she said. "That man is in love with you. I've never seen it before, in him, but there it is."

Amy just shook her head. Aunt Bridget was matchmaking, that's all.

They were distracted by Jamie piling porridge beside his bowl for his horsey to eat, and the subject was dropped as they cleaned up the mess.

After lunch, Rory's carriage arrived once again to take her to the office. Jamie hugged her good-bye but Susan quickly distracted him with a game of peck-a-boo and Amy slipped away, anxious to be at work.

And so their days fell into a routine.

The hard part of the day, for Amy, was after dinner. The light in the cottage at night was not adequate for easy reading. Rory stopped by one night to say good-night and saw this, and the next night invited her to bring her book into his library, where the light was better. Jamie could play on the floor while she read.

And so a new ritual started. After supper, they all would go into the library, where a warm fire blazed, and they would read their books. Rory bought some picture books for Jamie and he seemed happy to look at them for a while, pointing out cows and sheep and chickens for them.

One night, Rory heard Amy sniffing and saw her dabbing her eyes with her handkerchief. Was she ill?

"Are you all right?" he asked.

Amy looked sheepish.

"I'm just reading a book by Miss Louisa May Alcott," she said. "It's called, *Little Women*, and it's quite sad. One of the sisters dies. It reminds me that I always wanted a sister myself. My mother had a difficult birth with me and could not have more children. Being an only child, my best playmates were always books. But I sometimes pretended I had a sister. I named her Maisie. Don't ask me why."

Rory looked at her oddly.

"I'm an only child, too, you know. I always wanted a brother. My father died before my mother could have more children and she never remarried. I used to pretend I had a brother—when I was little, of course. But I didn't name him. I just called him Brother. We had all kinds of adventures in my head! As for books, I found them good company when I was at sea."

And there it was. Another bond between them.

Jamie had started falling asleep on the rug in front of the fire, so Rory picked him up and carried him to the cottage. Amy and Rory tucked him in his cot—though he would not stay there the whole night yet. Before morning, he would be crawling into Amy's bed snuggling close for comfort.

She walked Rory to the door and stepped outside into the crisp autumn evening air. The stars were glittering brightly and she looked up at them.

Then he kissed her.

At first, she was surprised, but then she felt herself kissing him back. Desire rose in her so strong it almost brought her to her knees. Rory pressed himself against her, murmured something to himself, then pulled away.

"I told you, I dishonored you once," he said. "I won't do it again. But you really should think about marrying me, if nothing else to put me out of my misery."

With that, he turned and walked back to the house.

CHAPTER NINE

He began to court her in earnest. There was no other explanation. When he seated her at the table, he would lightly press her shoulder before moving to his own chair. When he helped her out of a carriage, he held her hand just a moment too long. He touched her—lightly, fleetingly, every chance he got.

Mondays, when she returned home to her cottage from work, fresh flowers were on her kitchen table. When she asked Aunt Bridget about it, the older woman just shrugged, but there was a twinkle in her eye.

One morning, at breakfast, Aunt Bridget announced they were going to the dressmaker's.

"Susan can watch Jamie this morning and we will go get you a few new things," Aunt Bridget announced.

"I'm fine," Amy started to object.

"I am sick to death of those skirts and shirtwaists," the older woman said. "You need some appropriate attire for work and for entertaining."

"Entertaining?" Amy repeated. "What entertaining?"

"Well, the holidays are coming up and we usually have at least one house party, plus we are invited to several others."

Aunt Bridget said, seeming determined.

"But surely I won't be included in those," Amy protested. "I'm not family."

"You most certainly are!" Aunt Bridget retorted. "We won't force you to attend other parties, but we would be remiss if we did not include you in our own, at least. You are, after all, our houseguest, if nothing else."

Amy had begun to learn that, despite her petite stature, Aunt Bridget had a will of iron.

"My parents will be here in a few weeks with some of my better clothes," Amy said. "Can't we wait until then?"

It was as if she hadn't spoken.

"The carriage will be out front in an hour. Be ready," she called as she left the room.

Amy felt ambushed, but she had to laugh. The older woman was indeed a force to be reckoned with.

When they got to the dressmaker's, Madame Marie clapped her hands and admired Amy's tall, slender figure.

"It will be such fun to dress you!" she exclaimed. She busily took measurements and wrote down notes in a little notebook.

"Rose, I think, is a good color for you," she announced. "And jewel tones. With that dark hair and creamy skin, yes!"

When they left the shop, Amy's head was whirling. All the fabrics that had been swished over her body, the flying hands of Madame Marie, the rapid-fire exchanges between the seamstress and Aunt Bridget, had left her breathless. Growing up, her mother had made most of her clothes. It was a rare treat to go to a seamstress.

Madame Marie promised the clothes within a week.

That afternoon, when she left the shipping office, Rory

handed her an envelope.

"Your pay," he announced. "We pay employees once a month."

Amy tucked it into her reticule and didn't look until she got home. When she opened it, she was stunned. After her lightkeeper's pay, it was an astonishing amount. Within a few months, she should be able to afford to be independent, to find her own lodgings. She was surprised that the thought didn't please her more.

When the bright pink boxes arrived a week later from Madame Marie, Aunt Bridget helped her open them. There was a lovely rose wool dress, a tailored emerald green frock suitable for work, and a stunning teal blue velvet dress with a heart-shaped neckline.

"This is too much!" Amy protested.

Aunt Bridget shushed her.

"It's just a few nice things, for special occasions," she said. "Rory picked out the velvet, as an early Christmas present."

Amy was stunned that he involved himself in something as mundane as her wardrobe. She had never known a man to do that. Certainly, her father never advised her mother on what to wear—and Reuben barely paid any attention to her attire.

That night, before dinner, she took Rory aside and thanked him.

"It wasn't necessary," she said, "But it's a lovely gown. Thank you."

He was pleased, if a little embarrassed to be caught ordering women's fashions.

"With what you are paying me, I can afford to buy my own clothes now," she added, and went to put Jamie in his high chair.

That night, Uncle Seamus showed up for dinner. He had

left on a business trip right after she arrived and she had not had much opportunity to get to know him. He seemed tired, after weeks of visiting seaports to drum up business for the shipping company, and excused himself after dinner and went straight to bed.

The next morning, she was lingering over breakfast and a cup of tea with Aunt Bridget when the older man came downstairs.

He sat down at the far end of the table after helping himself to a substantial plateful, and began to eat silently. Aunt Bridget went to the kitchen to discuss lunch and dinner menus and left Amy, Jamie and Uncle Seamus alone.

When he didn't speak, Amy felt obliged to make some conversation.

"Was your business trip successful?" she asked.

He nodded but kept eating.

"Traveling can be very wearying," she offered, thinking of the two-day coach ride to Boston from Port Smythe.

Again, he nodded and made a noise that sounded something like a grunt. He finished his food, wiped his mouth with his napkin, stood up and said, "Excuse me," and made a little bow. Then he was gone.

Amy was baffled. The man had been just shy of rude. Certainly not friendly. Had she done something to offend him? Then Jamie began to squirm to get down from the table and she was distracted. But later that day, when she was at the office, Seamus walked by the open door to the accountants' office and didn't even look in.

Maybe he was just the surly sort, she thought, until she heard him laughing with Rory in the other office. Maybe it was just her, she finally concluded. He didn't like her.

The next morning, Uncle Seamus was gone before Amy arrived for breakfast, and most days after that. At dinner, he was usually quiet unless a family member spoke to him, and he pleaded exhaustion every night after dinner and retreated to his room.

Amy didn't have time to pursue the problem, between taking care of Jamie in the mornings and making sure he didn't feel abandoned, and working in the afternoons. Besides, her parents were coming to visit before winter set in and she wanted to plan some outings with them.

They arrived one week in early November, and her mother had packed a trunkful of Amy's better clothes that she had left at home when she went to work at the lighthouse.

They were awful.

She did not remember how childish some of her things were until she measured them against the more sophisticated things she had been wearing. Puffed sleeves and ruffles no longer suited her. She found one or two suitable garments, but decided most of them would be offered to Susan. The girl had few clothes and was young enough that these dresses would suit her just fine, if shortened. She did not tell her mother, but Margaret Bennett had already discerned that Amy was wearing much more elegant gowns than the ones a mother had so lovingly sewn.

Her parents seemed concerned when they first arrived, but seeing her ensconced in the guest cottage soothed their fears somewhat. They noted the solicitous way Rory treated their daughter, and they fell in love with Aunt Bridget.

Their first night at the Fitzgerald mansion, Amy invited them to the cottage after dinner for a private visit.

"Is he going to marry you?" her mother asked, bluntly.

"He's asked, but I don't know," Amy said. "He says he wants to do the right thing by me. He says he wants to be a father to Jamie. He says he owes me his life. In my book, those aren't good enough reasons to get married."

"Whyever not?" her mother asked, astonished.

"I was married once and Reuben was as good a husband as he knew how to be," Amy said, "but I don't want to just 'make do,' if you know what I mean. I just don't think that duty and obligation are good enough reasons to marry."

"Well, he's obviously rich—you should see our guest room! He's handsome by any standard, though his hair is a little long and … very bright. He's a successful businessman. And he seems to dote on you and Jamie, or at least treat you well. What more could you want?"

Amy sighed.

"Just … more," she said.

And she changed the subject to what they would be doing the next day. She would take her parents on the same tour Rory had taken her on when she first arrived, introducing them to the city's landmarks and history. She had read more about Boston's history and thought they would find it as interesting as she did.

Her father had been fairly quiet through all the conversation and that night, when they got home, he found Amy giving Jamie a bedtime snack in the kitchen. Jamie had become great friends with Mrs. Fiona Lafferty, the cook, and she made him special treats each night. Tonight, it was hot cocoa and buttered toast.

Her father walked into the kitchen and sat down at the table.

"How are you taking all this?" he asked. "You seem happy enough."

"I am content," Amy replied. She stirred her own cocoa, then looked at him.

"Do you remember when I left for the lighthouse, you gave me a book of essays by Mr. Emerson? It took me a while to read them, but when I did, I was fascinated by the one called 'Self Reliance.' Mr. Emerson talked about being true to one's self, not letting society tell us how to live our lives.

"I'm not sure I understood or agreed with everything he had to say, but I did take a lesson from it. I taught myself to swim. I learned to fish for my dinner. I grew my own food. I did a hard job. And when Jamie happened, I took responsibility for him.

"I won't deny Rory the right to be a father to him, but neither will I let him convince me to marry him because it's the 'right thing to do.' I need more than that. I let you and Mother and Reuben talk me into marrying the first time, but this time it will be my decision."

Her father started to protest. "We just wanted the best ..."

"Hush," Amy interrupted him, surprised at herself. "I don't blame you. You thought it was best for me then. But now, I decide what's best for me. And I'm not sure what that is right now."

Her father looked at her with a new respect.

"You know your mother and I both love you and want nothing more than your happiness," her father replied. "I hope you find it. And for what it's worth, I think he's a fine man. Your mother thinks he's quite a catch.

"Meanwhile, I'm going to take this opportunity to tuck in my grandson for the night," he said, swooping up a delighted Jamie into his arms and preceding Amy to the cottage.

After her parents left, things fell back into their happy routine.

When Amy got her next pay envelope, she broached the subject that had been worrying her.

"I can't keep this lying around my cottage. How can I open a bank account?" she asked Rory.

"Your father was a banker!" he responded. "So I thought you would have figured it out. We'll go to the bank tomorrow and open an account for you."

True to his word, the next day they went to Rory's bank. He had barely walked in the door and the bank president came scuttling out of his office, happy to see his favorite customer.

"Captain Fitzgerald! So good to see you looking well after your unfortunate incident," the banker said. He turned to Amy. "And who is your charming companion?"

"Amy, this is Mr. Phineas Tucker, president of the bank," Rory said. "And this is Mrs. Amy Pritchard, a new employee of mine. She is helping Simon with the accounting, and she needs to open a bank account. She's new in town."

Mr. Tucker bowed briefly over Amy's hand and led them to his own office. A quick bit of paperwork and Amy had her own account, from which she could draw cash or write draughts.

"You're working with Simon, then?" the banker asked, as they were leaving. "What are you doing for him?"

Amy explained, briefly. Tucker looked amazed.

"A woman," he marveled. "Doing ciphers and checking Simon Trask's work. I never heard of such a thing!"

Rory intervened before Amy could come back with a sharp retort.

"If you recall, Mr. Tucker, my mother has helped my grandfather run Shamrock Shipping for many years now," he said. "She doesn't just decorate the office, I guarantee you."

Tucker had the grace to blush a little and stammered his apologies.

As they left, Rory took Amy's arm and guided her down the steps of the bank.

"I thought I'd save him from you," he laughed. "You should have seen your face. One of these days, I'll tell him about your lightkeeper career and how you saved my life. That should shut him up."

Amy had to laugh then, too, and suddenly the day seemed full of promise. She had her own bank account! Could independence be far away? But not yet, she told herself. She wanted a healthy nest egg before she struck out on her own.

CHAPTER TEN

The next week, it rained incessantly. Jamie was restless and Amy was feeling claustrophobic when, on Sunday morning, the day dawned bright and clear.

At breakfast, Rory suggested they go for a carriage ride down to the wharf after he returned from escorting his aunt to Mass. Uncle Seamus was out of town again.

After a light lunch at home, they set out. When they arrived at dockside, Jamie was beside himself with excitement. He pointed at the large ships in port, wanting to know what they were. His favorite new word was "whassat?" He wanted names for everything.

"It's a ship," Rory said.

"Sip," Jamie repeated. "Big sip!"

They wandered the docks for a while, watching men working, even on the Sabbath, loading vessels with cargo.

"When will your new ship be ready?" Amy asked.

Rory paused, as if calculating.

"In the spring," he said. "She's going to be a beauty."

They drove to an overlook to see the Boston lighthouse, called the Boston Light by locals. Perched out on Little Brewster Island in Boston Harbor, it stood sentinel, and

Amy could see there was a little white cottage next to it, along with a few outbuildings. It was much more isolated than her lighthouse at Point Peril, she thought. Looking at it gave her a sense of longing, though. She rather missed her lighthouse.

Rory could see that, and promised that one day, when the weather got nice in the spring, they would row over to the lighthouse and visit it. That seemed to make her happy.

"You know, it was the first lighthouse built in the United States," he told her. "This one replaced the original one and was built almost 100 years ago."

It was a lovely afternoon and Amy was sad to see it end. Jamie fell asleep on the way home, but for days afterwards he wanted to go again to see the "sips."

In early December, Amy learned that Rory's mother, the venerable Mollie Kathleen herself, was coming to visit for Christmas.

"It's not a great time of year for the crossing, but since I wrote and told her about you and Jamie, she's been dying to come meet you both," Rory said, casually.

Amy felt a shiver of … fear? Meeting the formidable Mrs. Fitzgerald was going to be daunting. What would the woman think of her? She pictured an iron-corseted virago, something like Mrs. Agatha Bean, but tougher. Everyone talked about her with such awe.

Now that she had some money of her own, Amy decided to go shopping for Christmas.

She bought Rory a pair of fine leather driving gloves. Aunt Bridget would get a pretty brooch of a four-leaf clover set with green stones. She got Uncle Seamus a soft blue woolen scarf, since he always seemed to be cold, but she was unsure of her purchase. Would he like anything she gave him, she wondered?

She bought a few toys for Jamie. She sent sachets to her mother and a book to her father. Anticipating that Rory's mother might also be there, she bought a pearl-edged comb for her hair—simple, but elegant.

Her purchases snugly tucked beside her in the carriage, she took them home to hide until December 25th.

But there was one hurdle to overcome before the holiday: The annual Fitzgerald Christmas party.

Rory and his aunt and uncle were invited to several house parties in the weeks before Christmas, but Amy refused to go.

"They don't know me and I'm not really invited," she insisted. "And I don't know them. Our situation is somewhat awkward and hard to explain, you have to admit, and polite conversation will hardly cover it."

For once, she stood her ground with Aunt Bridget, and Rory reluctantly acceded to her wishes.

"But you must promise me you'll come to our own party," he asked her. "I'll be discreet when I introduce you."

The day of the dinner party, just a few days before Christmas, the house was abuzz with servants, some hired just for the occasion. A table was set in the long hall for thirty dinner guests. There was a giant wreath on the front door and a smaller one on her cottage door. The biggest Christmas tree she had ever seen was set up and decorated in the mansion's entry hall. Jamie was ecstatic over it.

The night of the party, she wore the teal velvet dress. Its simple lines and sweetheart neckline showed her slim figure to its best advantage. She had bought herself teal-dyed leather slippers to match, and Aunt Bridget insisted it needed some jewelry in the neckline. She found a simple string of pearls that went perfectly with it and loaned them to Amy. The maid that Aunt Bridget used for such occasions also did Amy's hair in a chignon that looked very sophisticated, especially when she tucked a pearl comb into it.

Amy looked at herself in the cottage mirror and marveled that it was indeed her looking back. She had never dressed in such elegant finery.

Her entrance into the house, after Jamie hugged her good-night and Susan assured her she should stay as late as she wanted, was greeted by silence.

Rory stood staring at her as if he'd never seen her before. Aunt Bridget, also decked out in her holiday finery, was for once speechless. But not for long.

"My, my, girl, you do dress up fine," she said. "You look lovely as a blue sky after a week of fog."

"Indeed," Rory added, and whispered to her as they entered the ballroom, "You look stunning."

Soon, guests began to arrive and Amy was separated from Rory and his aunt and found herself on her own. She tried to hide in a corner by some ferns, but people kept seeking her out.

She stuck to the houseguest story, saying she was a widow and now working for the shipping company, and that the situation was temporary, commenting pointedly on how comfy the guest cottage was.

The most uncomfortable part of the evening was watching Rory with a business associate, a Mr. O'Donnell, and the man's daughter, Dorothy ("call me Dotty"). Cute little Dotty rushed forward as soon as they were in the room and latched onto Rory, clinging to his arm and flashing her fine eyes at him every chance she got.

Amy felt a rush of something—anger, jealousy? She had

no right to those feelings, she knew, but they were there just the same. Rory kept trying to work his way over to her, but couldn't get more than a few feet before being accosted by some other guest. It was obvious he was well-liked. Dotty never left his side.

Finally, he made his way to the corner and introduced the two women. Again, they used the new employee-widow-houseguest strategy, but Dotty wasn't buying it. She kept looking at Amy suspiciously, eyeing her tall, slender figure with dislike.

First Uncle Seamus, now this woman, she thought. *What have I done to gain their enmity?*

When supper was announced, Rory said something Amy didn't hear over the din of conversation, turned and walked away with Dotty on his arm. Amy didn't know what to do. Then he presented the young woman to her father and returned to Amy, offering his arm to her.

"Dine with me?" he asked. Amy almost felt faint with relief. Dotty cast glaring looks her way all through dinner. Amy ignored her. That night, Rory walked Amy back to the cottage after everyone had gone. Snow was falling lightly, so he removed his jacket and put it around her shoulders for the short walk. At the door, he once again kissed her, but lightly, hesitantly, and wished her good night. Amy reluctantly admitted to herself that she felt disappointed.

Two days later, on Christmas Eve, Mollie Kathleen Fitzgerald arrived. Her ship had been delayed by inclement weather, but she made it just in time for the holiday celebration. Rory drove down to the docks to fetch her and when they came back to the house, she went to her room to rest and "freshen up."

Dinner was festive, with a huge roast of beef and potatoes and a grand trifle concocted by Mrs. Lafferty. But the highlight of the evening was the arrival of the daunting Mrs. Fitzgerald, who appeared after everyone was gathered, having pre-dinner drinks. She was nearly as tall as Amy, with a still-fine figure and flaming hair threaded with silver.

She hugged her son, brother and sister-in-law, then turned to Amy.

"And this must be Amy, the fine girl who saved my son's life," she said. "I can never thank you enough."

She took Amy's hand and pulled her into a warm hug.

"And where is my beautiful grandson?" she asked.

"I'm afraid he was tired and went to bed early," Amy said, "but you'll see him in the morning. Mrs. Flannery made him something special for dinner and Susan is with him now, Mrs. Fitzgerald."

"Oh, darlin', call me Mollie," Rory's mother said. "Let's not be formal at this point."

Amy liked her. A lot. And was so relieved.

On Christmas morning, Amy wore her rose wool dress and took special care with Jamie's attire. His grandmother bent down to introduce herself and even though Jamie was shy, he seemed to take to her. Mollie knew enough to give him some space.

"He's a lovely boy," she said to Amy, echoing Aunt Bridget's words. "And you have done a good job with him. He's so well-behaved!"

After breakfast, they all gathered in the drawing room by a smaller tree to exchange gifts. Rory was beaming over his leather driving gloves and was so touched, Amy wished she had bought him something nicer. Jamie got new clothes from her parents and also from Aunt Bridget and Uncle Seamus. He needed them, he was growing so fast.

Uncle Seamus seemed surprised and pleased at her gift, but only offered a curt thanks, and Aunt Bridget loved her brooch. Mollie loved her pearl comb.

Jamie was thrilled when he opened the gift from his father—a hand-carved wooden ship complete with canvas sails and lots of detail. "Big sip!" he dubbed it.

Rory's mother gave her a lovely tatted lace collar from Ireland. It would dress up her work attire and she would wear it a lot. Then Rory handed her two small packages. In the first was a scent called "Sea Rose" that did indeed take her back to the roses that grew on the sea wall by the lighthouse. The other was a small jewelry box containing a silver pendant on a fine silver chain. The pendant was a mermaid. Delicately wrought in silver, the mermaid was chastely robed in flowing hair.

"I had it made," Rory said. Their eyes met, and Amy blushed. Luckily, everyone seemed to be busily exclaiming over their own gifts, and no one seemed to notice her face getting pink. Or at least that's what she hoped.

Christmas dinner was roast goose and everyone seemed ready to relax afterward. By the end of the afternoon, Jamie was sitting on Mollie's lap, talking about his toy ship and presumably recounting, in toddler language, their trip to the docks.

It was the first Christmas without her parents, yet she felt like she had found a second family with the Fitzgeralds. Most of them, anyway.

CHAPTER ELEVEN

After Christmas, a new face showed up at the door of the Fitzgerald home one evening during dinner. The door chimes rang and a maid came to tell Rory that he had a visitor in the library.

Rory left, excusing himself, and in a few minutes everyone in the dining room heard a ruckus outside. There was shouting and back-slapping and laughter. Aunt Bridget looked annoyed.

"You didn't tell me Thomas came over on the ship with you," she said to Mollie.

Mollie laughed.

"Well, you know Thomas. If there's peace and quiet anywhere, he's bound and determined to stir things up. I was hoping he'd spare us for a few more days."

Soon, the two men entered the dining room. Rory asked the maid to let Mrs. Flannery know they had an extra guest for dinner.

Rory introduced his cousin, Thomas O'Brien, also a nephew to Bridget and Seamus. He was almost as tall as Rory, with crow-black hair and bright blue eyes.

"Well, well," he said when Rory introduced Amy. "Now I

know why cuz was so eager to get back to the states."

Rory punched his cousin lightly on the shoulder.

"Back off, *cuz*," he said. "Mrs. Pritchard is a respectable lady and you're not to be so familiar with her."

"I wouldn't dream of it," Thomas said, and sat down to a plate of food just brought from the kitchen. Questions about his current state of affairs followed from family members. Amy excused herself before dessert and fled to her cottage.

Later that evening, as she strained to read by the dim light of the cottage, Rory knocked at the door. She met him in the doorway but did not invite him in.

"Jamie's already asleep," she said. "I'm afraid you missed saying good-night."

"Sorry," Rory said. "I got caught up with Thomas, reminiscing, and lost track of time. I hope he didn't offend you."

"He's quite … energetic," Amy said. "And brash. I'm not sure I like him much."

Rory laughed.

"Thomas is an acquired taste," he admitted. "But he'll grow on you."

He started to leave, then turned back.

"Oh, just so you know, I'm going out tomorrow night with him, for old time's sake. I likely won't be home till late. I'll miss spending the evening with you, though."

Then he was gone into the darkness of the garden.

Amy had to admit she was disappointed. She had got used to having evenings with him. But, she thought, she should get accustomed to it, because when she got her own house, she would not see him nearly so much. And they certainly would not be spending cozy evenings by the fire.

The next day, she barely saw him at all. She had just arrived at the office after lunch when he left, leather portfolio tucked under his arm. She was more than curious about its contents by now, though likely it was just business-related papers and such.

That afternoon, his first mate, Roscoe, showed up at the office, looking for the captain. Amy saw him wandering the hall and, knowing Rory was out, asked if he needed assistance.

The sailor looked hard at her and asked: "Are ye the lady what saved Cap'n Fitz? I heered you worked here."

Amy blushed and admitted she was the one.

"I been meanin' to meet ye," he said. "First, I gotta thank ye for savin' me cap'n's life. He's a right good bloke. And I got a story to tell ye, what ye might be interested in, bein' a lady lightkeeper and all."

Amy assured him she'd like to hear the story.

"Seems there was this couple, man an' wife like, who tended a lighthouse up in Maine. The feller died and his wife didn't have nowhere's else to go, so she buried him quiet-like and didn't tell nobody he croaked. She tended the lighthouse all by hersel' for two more years afore they figgered it out. She done such a good job, they let her keep on."

"Is she still there?" Amy asked, curious.

"Nope. She finally got too old to do the work and retired. Story goes, her sister's husband had died in the meantime, so she went to live with her in the end. Amazin', though, ain't it?"

Amy smiled.

"Yes, amazing," she agreed.

Then she told the first mate that Rory was at the shipyard, and that he could find him there. Roscoe tipped his hat and thanked her, then left, whistling. Amy couldn't wait to tell Rory the story, then remembered he would not be home tonight. It seemed odd to have him absent. Just think how much she would miss him when he went on his next voyage. It made her incredibly sad.

That night, after dinner, she had to convince Jamie to go back to the cottage right away. He liked their routine, too. Mollie was at a friends' house for dinner and Aunt Bridget had retired early with a headache. Uncle Seamus was once again out of town. So Amy would have felt strange going into the library without a family member present. It still seemed presumptuous.

Later that night, she awoke when she heard a carriage arrive, and two men singing what seemed to be bawdy songs. She decided they had been drinking and that Thomas was not a good influence on his cousin.

The next morning, at breakfast, Rory seemed to be feeling under the weather. He had not gone to the office early, as was his custom. He drank a lot of coffee and ate a few pieces of toast, but still looked green.

"Did you have a nice evening with Thomas?" she asked, to be polite.

He gave her a warning look and she did not pursue the subject.

That night, they read in silence and Jamie looked from one to the other as if wondering why. Rory fell asleep in his chair by the fire and Amy took her son to the cottage without waking his father.

The following day, things went back to normal. Except Rory came home for lunch, because he had forgotten his leather portfolio, and so they had lunch together and the conversation stayed on light subjects.

After lunch, before the carriage arrived to take her to the

office, Jamie played his "hide-and-seek" game with her. He disappeared out of the dining room while she was chatting with Mrs. Lafferty. Amy went to look for him and heard the sound of a piano being plinked off-key. She followed it and found herself in a small, but lovely, music room with a perfectly wonderful piano.

Soon, Rory came looking for them both and heard the opening strains of "Moonlight Sonata" being picked out on the piano. He came to the doorway and found Amy playing it, tentatively. Jamie sat by her on the piano bench and listened, fascinated. This was a new trick his mother had revealed.

"Lovely," Rory said, applauding lightly, and Amy shot to her feet, as if caught doing something wrong.

"I'm sorry," she said. "I was looking for Jamie and found him here. He does tend to wander."

"Don't be sorry," Rory said. "It was very nice. Play some more."

"Oh, I haven't played in a long time. My parents had me take lessons for years but I never got very good at it, I'm afraid. After Rebecca died, I quit playing altogether. And I didn't exactly have a piano at the lighthouse."

"Well, we'll have to vary our evenings so you can play for me—and Jamie—once in a while. My mother plays, but I haven't heard her do so in a long time, either."

His mother had been engaged with a round of social events since her return, "catching up with friends," as she put it. But that next night, at dinner, she put in an appearance, and Rory mentioned Amy's piano skills. Over Amy's initial protests, they finally decided to spend an evening in the music room. Jamie loved it, and danced to even the slowest tune. The two women laughed at their mistakes, and Amy felt more relaxed and closer to Mollie than she had so far.

Now if she could just win over Uncle Seamus.

Amy's chance to speak with Uncle Seamus came one January morning when everyone else had left the table but her and Jamie, who was busily concentrating on his breakfast. The older man was unusually late for breakfast, having just returned the night before from yet another business trip.

"How was your trip?" Amy inquired.

Uncle Seamus shrugged and kept on eating.

Amy decided polite wasn't the way to go. She might as well be bold. It wasn't going to hurt their relationship, she thought.

"Why don't you like me?" she asked, bluntly.

Uncle Seamus went still. He swallowed and wiped his mouth with a napkin.

"I like you fine," he grumbled. But he kept looking at his plate.

"No, you don't," Amy persisted. "You don't talk to me, you don't look at me, and you avoid me whenever possible. What did I do to offend you?"

The older man was at a loss for words at first. Then he looked straight at Amy. Honesty deserved honesty.

"Why won't you marry my nephew?" he asked. "He not good enough for you? Being Irish and all? I've seen it before. He's a good-looking fellow, smart and educated—not always the same thing, you know. He's learning to run the business, knows the way of the ships and crews, more than I did at his age. He'll be a good provider. And he dotes on the boy. Fond of you, too. I can tell."

Amy was taken aback by the speech, the most words

she had ever heard come out of the man's mouth since she had met him.

"I don't know where to begin," she said, hesitantly. "I assume he's told you about how we met and what happened that night. We both made a mistake and he should not have to pay for it."

"It has nothing to do with being Irish. It has nothing to do with being a good provider. I lost one husband in the war, and a child thereafter. I have lost enough people dear to me to be cautious. Being a sea captain is a dangerous profession —proof being in how we met! I'm not ready to risk that again.

"I have come to care for and admire Rory, and I think he feels the same about me, but shouldn't marriage be based on more than that? What if we marry out of obligation and then he meets the love of his life? What then?"

It was Uncle Seamus' turn to be surprised.

"I didn't know all that," he said. He cleared his throat, obviously uncomfortable. "I'm sorry if I misjudged you. Can we start over?"

Amy smiled, and went to him, giving him a light hug.

"Oh, yes, please," she said.

Jamie climbed down from his high chair and ran to the man and hugged him, too, which made Seamus smile and pat the boy's head. "Cute little tyke," he said. "Reminds me of his father at that age. Smart, too."

Jamie was happy to make a new friend. It was another person he could hug. It was his latest discovery—hugging people other than his mother.

Not having spent much time around other children in his life, he was especially fascinated by people his own size. He would go up to strange children in the shops and hug them. Not something which all children liked. More than once, Amy had to apologize to a surprised mother for her son's affectionate behavior.

Which may be how he caught the influenza going around Boston that winter.

CHAPTER TWELVE

One night, Amy arrived home from work and found Susan hovering anxiously in the cottage doorway, watching for her.

"What is it?" Amy asked, as soon as she saw the girl's face.

"I'm not sure," Susan said. "But Jamie's not feeling well. I think he has a fever and he's cranky, which he rarely is. He's been sleeping most of the afternoon. You should look in on him."

Amy quickly threw her cloak and bonnet on the settee in her sitting room and went to her son. He was sleeping, but flushed and warm. He had kicked off his covers.

"I looked for Aunt Bridget, but she was out for the afternoon, and Mrs. Lafferty just got back from the market," Susan said. "I didn't know what to do."

Amy tamped down the panic that was rising in her. She knew influenza was raging through the city, and had tried to limit contact with the general public. She kept thinking about Rebecca and fought the mounting fear.

She could not bear to lose her sweet boy. She asked Susan to fetch Mrs. Lafferty, some cloths and a basin of cool water. She remembered the willow bark tea Bess had given her—the same tea she had used for Rory when he became ill. When Mrs. Lafferty came, Amy gave her some of the tea and asked her to brew it for Jamie.

When Rory arrived home for dinner a bit later, he immediately came to the cottage to see what he could do. He could clearly see Amy's distress and it scared him. She was always so calm in a crisis—didn't he of all people know that? If she was scared, then he was terrified for his son.

They took turns in the evening tending to the boy, trying to keep his temperature down. They poured sweetened, warm tea down his throat, which had taken on a raspy sound. They did everything they could. Rory went to fetch the family doctor, who came about midnight.

"There's not much else you can do but what you are already doing," the doctor said. "I'll check back tomorrow."

They spent the entire next day tending to Jamie, and although everyone wanted to help, Amy told Aunt Bridget and Uncle Seamus to stay away for fear of catching the illness. Rory had to almost physically restrain his mother, who also wanted to tend the child.

"Amy, Susan and I have been exposed already," he said. "Mrs. Lafferty didn't have direct contact with him, so she should be fine. But for now we'll quarantine ourselves here to avoid spreading it. Please do this, Mother."

Reluctantly, Mollie agreed but called her love to the boy before she left.

Jamie didn't hear. He battled the fever for two days and nights while his attendants took turns caring for him. On the third night, exhaustion finally forced Amy to lie down on her bed. Susan was keeping watch. Rory was in the sitting room, rocking silently in Amy's chair before the fire.

When Amy woke with the morning rays of sun coming through the window, the cottage was silent. Too silent. Jamie was not whimpering. He also was not on the cot in his tiny bedroom. Her heart nearly stopped as a panicked Amy flung off the blanket covering her and staggered to her feet, still groggy with sleep. Where was her son? She stumbled into the sitting room. Susan was asleep on the settee, with Rebecca's quilt thrown over her. Rory sat in the rocking chair, Jamie asleep on his shoulder. He looked up when she entered and put a finger to his lips.

"It's the only way he'll sleep," he whispered. "The fever broke a few hours ago."

Amy nearly fainted with relief. She sat in the chair opposite the rocker, put her face in her hands and wept with relief. Rory wanted to comfort her, but didn't want to disturb the boy. Truth be told, he felt like crying with relief himself.

Jamie woke an hour or so later and said, 'Hungry, Papa." Amy rushed over, picked him up and hugged him tightly.

"Hungry, Mama," he demanded. Susan woke, hearing them, and also hugged the boy, then ran to the kitchen to get Mrs. Lafferty to make her charge some porridge with raisins and maple syrup.

The doctor came by later and checked Jamie, saying he should fully recover.

"He's a strong lad," the physician said, "and I think he got very good care."

He also wanted to know what was in Bess' tea.

After that, Amy would often picture the sight of Rory holding his son to his shoulder, rocking in front of the fire. It made her smile and feel truly safe for the first time in a long time.

Thomas put in frequent but sporadic appearances at the house, and was shocked to hear about the boy's illness. He expressed his sympathy. But when he asked Rory to go out for a night on the town, Rory declined.

"You're getting to be a stick in the mud, cuz," Thomas told him. Rory just laughed.

Rory later told Amy: "I'd rather spend an evening with you and Jamie than a night on the town, drinking and gambling and carousing with my cousin. It's time we both settled down, but I think it's going to take a while longer for Thomas."

It was flattering, but she hoped she wasn't putting a damper on his real preferences. Perhaps he was just being nice.

Thomas also was being very nice. He flirted with Amy every time he saw her, despite the dark looks he got from Rory. Amy had never really flirted with anyone and knowing this was just some kind of adult play, sometimes flirted back. It was the only way she knew how to relate to him, he was such a frivolous soul. That made Rory get even more vigilant when the three of them were together.

Thomas was often invited to dinner by Aunt Bridget, who felt her nephew didn't get decent meals at the club where he liked to stay. When he arrived early one evening, before Rory got home, he found Amy and Jamie in the music room, playing the piano. He sauntered in and leaned on the piano, listening. Amy stopped playing and greeted him.

"Good evening, Thomas," she said. "You're early. Rory's not home yet."

"Not to worry," he replied, "It just gives me extra time alone with his lovely lady."

Amy felt uncomfortable. Thomas could tell, so he changed the subject.

"I have to tell you the most amazing story I heard," he said. "You were one of those lady lightkeepers, right?"

Amy said she had been.

"Well, at my club one night, I mentioned it and another gentleman told me a story about a lady lightkeeper down south somewhere who got hired to keep the lighthouse there. Big, burly gal, by all accounts. She could row a boat like anything.

"The story goes, some local boys tried to sail a boat that belonged to one of their fathers. They didn't know what they were doing and capsized the thing right off. The lady lightkeeper saw it and jumped in her rowboat and went out to rescue them. She got the two fellows into the boat and they were yelling at her to get them to shore when she saw their dog treading water like mad. Against their wishes, she rowed to the dog and pulled it into the boat, too.

"The boys were mad because there was a crowd gathering onshore, laughing at them. So when they hit the beach, the boys took off. They say the only one who thanked her was the dog, who licked her face before running after them."

They both were laughing when Rory entered the room. He glowered at his cousin and greeted Amy.

"You're early, cuz," he said to Thomas, frowning.

"Well, you're late. So I was entertaining the lovely Miss Amy in your absence," Thomas replied. "Hope you don't mind."

Rory did. But all he said was, "I believe dinner is being served."

He stepped around his cousin and took Amy's hand,

helping her rise from the piano bench. Then he picked up Jamie and took his little family into the dining room.

Thomas smiled. One of them needed a push, he thought. But he wasn't certain which one.

CHAPTER THIRTEEN

One night at dinner, Rory announced he had a surprise for Amy and his mother.

"That writer you both like, Louisa May Alcott, is giving a public talk in the Concord town hall on Friday night," he said. "I thought you ladies would like to go hear her."

The two women were delighted. Alcott seldom made public appearances, and they both admired her abolitionist and suffragette leanings. It turned out to be a blustery night, but with more wind than snow, so travel was not impeded. Wrapped in their wool cloaks, they all descended the carriage at the venue, glad they had arrived early enough to get decent seats. By the time Alcott spoke, the hall was packed.

Alcott spoke of the evils of slavery, how the Constitution guaranteed rights for all and how slave ownership was not only a violation of the intent of the law, but also simply immoral and indecent. She praised the suffrage movement and spoke about how she believed that when women got the right to vote, the country would change for the better.

On the carriage ride home, all three were lost in thought about what the soft-spoken writer had said. Though her voice was quiet, her message was passionate. It gave them a lot to think about.

Finally, Rory broke the silence.

"I don't think I ever told either of you this, but I once rescued some slaves who were escaping from their owners," he said. "We were sailing along the Carolina coast, just before the war broke out. We were holding close to shore because of squalls farther out, and we saw three Negroes running down the beach, waving at us.

"I had a couple of my men launch a lifeboat and row toward them. Before they reached the escapees, a group of white men broke out from the cover of the woods with dogs and guns. They started firing upon us! I could hear the dogs from the ship, but the animals were afraid to go into the ocean. We managed to get the men into the lifeboat and bring them to the ship safely.

"They were in terrible shape. Backs raw from whipping, clothes in rags, nearly starved to death and desperate for water. We took them with us back to Boston."

The women were silent for a while, then Amy asked: "What happened to them?"

"They all work in our shipyard," Rory said. "They live in the cottages we have for employees. Or at least two of them still live there. The third one met a woman, another escapee, working here in Boston as a maid at a hotel, and they got married. Now they have their own place, and two children."

Amy smiled.

"I like happy endings," she said, and Mollie reached for her hand in the semi-darkness of the carriage. She looked at Amy meaningfully. "So do I," she said.

Amy knew Mollie wanted her to marry Rory. But Mollie never mentioned it, except obliquely. Amy was beginning to think it might be time to move out of the guest cottage, but she kept finding reasons not to do so.

One night, as Rory carried a sleeping Jamie to the cottage and helped her put him to bed, he asked her to come outside and sit on the garden bench for a while.

It was a bright moonlit night, with no wind, but chilly as March can be. Amy brought her shawl.

As they sat on the bench, Rory casually put his arm along the back of the bench behind Amy's shoulders. They made small talk at first, about how Jamie was growing and how well he had recovered from his illness, about the lovely custard Mrs. Flannery had made for dessert, about how spring seemed to be in the air finally. Then Rory moved closer and addressed what was really on his mind.

"We need to talk about the night of the storm," he said.

Amy started to rise, but his arm tightened around her shoulders—enough so that she could not stand.

"Stay," he asked. "Please. We need to talk about it."

Amy shook her head.

"What happened, happened," she said. "You're under no obligation to me. I thought I made that clear."

"That's not what I want to talk about right now," he replied. "I need to know something."

He took a breath.

"Did I hurt you, that night?" he said.

"What?" Amy was dumbfounded. "No! We both almost died, but you did nothing to hurt me."

Rory started again.

"I mean, did I hurt you when we made love?" he asked.

Amy stared at him. Then, even in the moonlight, he

could see she was blushing. She looked down at her hands, lying in her lap.

"Not at all," she said quietly. "It was ... well, wonderful. I had never ... experienced ... anything like it."

Rory looked puzzled.

"But you were married. You had a child, so this was not entirely new to you."

Amy squirmed a bit, but he held her firmly.

"Well, of course, I had ... that ... with Reuben. But Reuben was a no-nonsense sort of man. His ... lovemaking, as you call it ... was rather ... perfunctory."

"Perfunctory?" Rory repeated. "Lass, your vocabulary always amazes me."

His voice softened and he kissed her lightly on the forehead.

"And I'm so sorry. You deserve so much more than that."

He slid his other arm around her waist and pulled her to him. He held her close.

"I hope you have a better word for my approach to the matter," he whispered into her ear.

Amy smiled, hidden by his shoulder.

"I would say your approach was much more ... adept."

Rory smiled, too.

"Adept, is it?" he repeated. "Not a very exciting word."

"But accurate," she responded. "And wonderful."

He held her silently for a while, musing about their conversation. Then he tilted her chin up and looked into her face.

"So why won't you marry me? We could become adept together."

This time, Amy succeeded in pulling away. She stood and wrapped her shawl tightly around her.

"Rory, I care so much for you, and Jamie loves you, but I won't marry a man who spends most of his time at sea, leaving us alone and risking his life every day. I couldn't bear it if something happened to you, but it would be worse yet if I were once again a widow with a child—or children—to raise. Alone.

"I should marry again, to give Jamie a stable home life and a father, but it won't be someone who takes such big risks and leaves us alone for months or more at a time.

"You're a sea captain. That's who you are. I won't ask you to change that. You'd always resent it."

Amy whirled away from him and ran into the cottage before he could reply.

Inside the cottage, Amy got ready for bed. It wasn't until she pulled her nightgown over her head that she realized tears were streaming down her face. She had to admit it. She loved Rory Fitzgerald. She waited for his touches, his purposefully brushing her shoulder in passing, his hand on her back as he guided her into the carriage. Her love also had become a longing, but common sense told her that she was making the right decision. Still, she cried until she fell asleep, her mermaid pendant clutched in her hand.

Out in the garden, Rory sat on the bench, chilled but unable to move. She said she couldn't bear it if something happened to him. She cared for him. He knew what he had to do, and he had to do it soon, before he lost her. But it was a big decision.

A FEW DAYS LATER, Amy left early for work and stopped by the book shop to find a volume of poetry by Emily Dickinson. She particularly liked the succinct sparseness of the woman's poems.

Mr. Wordsworth greeted her genially and helped her find the volume she sought.

"Captain Fitzgerald tells me you actually saved his life?" he asked, curiously. "How did you come to be a lightkeeper? It seems a strange profession for a gently reared young woman, though I've heard of others since then. If it's not too bold to ask, that is."

Amy gave him the short version and Wordsworth seemed fascinated.

He glanced toward the back of his shop, where a well-dressed gentleman was browsing through the shelves.

"There is someone I'd like you to meet," he said. The shopkeeper guided her to the back of the store, where said gentleman was perusing the non-fiction section.

"Mr. Harkness, I'd like you to meet Mrs. Amy Pritchard, new to Boston, with an interesting history you might like to know."

Amy was shocked for a moment, till she realized that the "history" was about her employment as a lightkeeper.

Harkness was a handsome man in his early 40s, perfectly groomed blond hair just beginning to show streaks of gray. He bowed slightly over her hand, and greeted her politely.

"Mrs. Pritchard was employed as a lightkeeper before she came to our fair city," Mr. Wordsworth explained.

Harkness showed immediate interest. And was full of questions.

He inquired: "How did you become a lightkeeper? Was it hard work for a woman?" and all the usual things people asked. But he seemed so keen on each answer that one question fed into another until she began to wonder what his motives were.

Finally, his questions stopped, and he explained his avid interest.

"I'm sorry, I've been quite rude," he said. "You must think I am insufferable! But I tell you, ma'am, that my interest is genuine. My partner and I own Harkness & Reed Publishing. We publish non-fiction books on current subjects. This is one that has held my interest since Mr. Wordsworth here first told me he'd met you."

"Did you actually save Captain Fitzgerald's life? How on earth were you able to do that? Oh, there I go again!"

Amy had encountered a lot of curiosity about her lightkeeper's job, but none so intense as this. She was flattered, but also a little nervous that he might uncover more than she really wanted him to know.

"Are you well educated then?" he asked, seeming to change subjects.

"Yes, I believe so. I went to a girls' school until I was seventeen and am well-read," she replied. She told him of her reading interests and he seemed particularly impressed that she had read Melville's lengthy tome twice.

"Have you any experience with writing?" he asked.

"Only a journal I kept as a girl," she said. "But I think I can spot good writing when I see it. I would like to write more, but my job and my young son keep me pretty well occupied."

"A son?" he asked. "Oh, you are married then?"

"No," Amy replied. "I am widowed." She didn't elaborate. Harkness smiled at her.

"What sort of job does a lovely young woman like you have now?" he asked.

"I'm a bookkeeper's assistant," she said. "I work for Captain Fitzgerald, in his office, checking Mr. Trask's work every day."

This brought raised eyebrows from Harkness.

"I never thought Simon Trask would allow such a thing," he remarked. "I've met him and he is a proud, and presumably very competent, man."

Amy explained about the older man's failing eyesight.

"Well, well, you are indeed a woman of many talents," Harkness said. "I salute you."

He eyed Amy curiously.

"Would you be willing to write something for me?" he asked.

"And what would that be?" Amy responded.

"Would you write a few pages of your story, about being a lightkeeper, so I can read it?"

"I can do that, but why?"

"I am thinking of a book now, something *avant garde*, about lady lightkeepers," he mused. "Do you know other lady lightkeepers? Or stories about them?"

"In fact, I haven't met any of the others, but I have heard a few tales," Amy said. "I probably could find more."

"Well, then, do we have a bargain? You will write something for me and I will decide if your skills are up to the task. I have a feeling they are. Your days as a bookkeeper's assistant might well be coming to an end."

Amy doubted it, but she smiled anyway. If nothing else, this might be fun.

After a bit more conversation, she left the store, a bounce in her step and anticipation in her heart.

Amy arrived at the office a few minutes late, uncharacteristic of her, and rushed into Rory's office to tell him the news.

He was not there, and she could hardly contain her disappointment. She was turning to leave when she saw his leather portfolio lying open on his desk. He usually kept it closed, and she could not suppress her curiosity. She walked over to the desk and looked down.

She could not believe her eyes. There, lying open on the desk in plain sight, was a charcoal sketch of her! She was standing at the sea wall, in her usual work skirt, bare feet and hair in a braid, looking out at the ocean, a faraway gaze in her eyes. It was such a startling likeness, she had no doubt as to who it was. She lifted the page and beneath it saw another sketch—of Jamie, playing with his wooden horsey in the grass by the base of the lighthouse. Then there was one of the lighthouse itself, with a faint figure standing on the parapet. Her again. And there was a close profile of her, much like the first drawing, but tightly focused on her face.

She caught her breath. Had Rory done these, and when? And why?

"That's private!" Rory said from the doorway, his voice tense. "Please put them back."

Amy dropped the drawings as if burned. Her face flamed with embarrassment at being caught.

"I'm so sorry," she said, still flustered. "I was looking for you and these were just lying here. Did you do these? They're very good. But when did you do them?"

Rory crossed the room and closed the folder briskly, looking to see which drawings she had observed.

"What did you think I did during the evenings after I left the lighthouse? Carouse at Port Smythe's many pubs? I did these in my room each evening. I like to draw. Always have. They're nothing.

"I also have work drawings in here, which is why I came back for the portfolio."

He looked at her curiously, no longer angry.

"Why were you looking for me?" he asked.

"It's nothing important," she said, still flustered. "I'll tell you this evening."

Then she turned and escaped into Simon Trask's office.

Rory wondered for a moment what was so important that she would come seek him out at work, which she rarely did, but he had an appointment to keep and needed to go.

That night, after dinner, when they went to the library, he brought it up.

"Why were you looking for me this afternoon?" he asked.

Amy paused for a minute, then looked at him.

"I've had an offer," she said.

"An offer?" he repeated.

"Well, today I was in Mr. Wordsworth's book shop and he introduced me to a man, a Mr. Harkness, who is a publisher here in Boston. Mr. Harkness wanted to know a bit about my experiences as a lightkeeper.

"I told him I wasn't the only one, that other women had done the same job for various reasons and in various circumstances. Besides my own experience, I told him what I had heard of other situations since then."

"You have?" Rory said, interested.

"One of your men—Roscoe—stopped by the office one day, looking for you, but ran into me," she said. "He asked me if I was the lady lightkeeper and I told him yes.

"Then he went on to tell me a story he heard about a woman in Maine whose husband died and who had nowhere else to go, so she didn't tell anyone he was dead and kept on running the lighthouse for two years before the service figured it out.

"She did such a good job, they kept her on till she couldn't do it anymore and retired."

Amy went on, undeterred by Rory's attentive silence.

She told him about the night when Thomas came to dinner and related the story of the boys in the sailboat, and how the dog was the only one who thanked her.

Rory sat there, just staring at her. Finally, he found speech.

"And what does all that have to do with this publisher fellow?" he inquired.

"He asked me if I would like to try to write a book on the subject of lady lightkeepers. We might call it *Ladies of the Lamp*. He's even going to loan me a typewriter. It's a new machine that some writers are using, instead of writing everything out in longhand. I'm going to teach myself to type!"

Rory was silent once again. This sounded dangerously like something that would give her the independence she craved—and that he dreaded. He shook off the feeling, knowing it was selfish.

"That's wonderful," he said, but she could sense the hesitancy in his reaction. She thought she understood exactly what he was thinking.

"It won't keep me from helping Simon," she promised. "But I may have to take a few trips to gather more stories. I can't write a book based solely on my experience and on hearsay."

Rory relaxed a little.

"We could take some trips together, if you like," he suggested, the idea forming as he spoke. "Uncle Seamus is getting tired of traveling to various port cities, drumming up business. I used to do some of that, but he took it over when I was indisposed. It's time I started doing my share again."

Amy eyed him suspiciously. She was too excited to question his motives right now. Maybe later.

That night, Rory urged Amy to share the news at dinner, and they all drank a toast to her new venture. If the couple harbored misgivings as to how this would affect their lives, they kept them to themselves.

CHAPTER FOURTEEN

April showers did indeed bring May flowers to Boston. The city suddenly burst into bloom, with flowering apple trees and brightly colored tulips at every turn. The new green leaves were almost iridescent, reminding Amy of the insides of some sea shells.

So she was in a happy mood as she exited the bank one afternoon after depositing her pay and keeping a bit of cash to buy Jamie some new clothes for the coming summer. He was growing so fast!

Rory had accompanied her, as he also had some business to attend to. As they were leaving, the bank manager called a greeting to Rory, and Rory politely stopped to chat with him for a minute.

"I'll meet you at the carriage," Amy said, eager to be out in the spring sunshine again. It had rained earlier in the day and the air was fresh and clean-smelling.

As she exited the bank, however, she ran smack into a man who was just entering. They both stepped back, apologizing, until they recognized each other.

"Reverend Snead!" Amy said. "What are you doing here?"

Snead's face twisted into a sour scowl.

"Well, if it isn't the whore of Point Peril," he sneered.

That was the last thing he said.

A fist shot past Amy's ear and hit the righteous reverend square in the face. He went down like a sack of potatoes and landed in a mud puddle, flat on his back. His mouth moved like a gasping fish, but no sound came out.

Amy whirled around, surprised.

"Rory!" she cried, as he stepped around her and loomed over the minister.

"Never. Speak. To. This. Woman. Again," he snarled. "Or you'll get worse than that."

Before Amy could react, he took her arm firmly and escorted her to the waiting carriage.

Inside, they were both quiet for a minute. Amy's first thought was to chastise him for punching the Reverend Snead. After all, he was a man of the cloth. But she couldn't help herself. She smiled. Then she giggled—something she rarely did. Then she laughed out loud. Rory joined her.

"I'm sorry," he said between chuckles. "I didn't mean to shock you. But he deserved it. And I don't think he'll bother you again."

Amy had no doubt. As they drove off, they saw the minister trying to rise, staggering with arms outstretched for balance, while passers-by made a broad berth around him.

Then Rory sobered.

"That's another reason we should marry," he said. "I can protect you from men like that."

So Amy told him the story of how she had handled the minister the first time he had accosted her. He laughed again, but not as hard as before.

"I stand corrected," Rory said. "I guess you don't need a

protector after all."

He said it graciously, but Amy thought he sounded disappointed. Then they dropped the subject.

She didn't see much of him in the following days. He seemed to be spending an inordinate amount of time at the shipyard. Was he avoiding her? She told herself that the new ship was almost ready and he probably was overseeing the final details before the launch.

One Saturday afternoon, when Rory was again at the shipyard, Mollie joined Amy and Jamie in the garden, where he was chasing butterflies, hopping after grasshoppers and generally fascinated with the new insect life there. They laughed at his antics until they heard thunder approaching, and took the child indoors to the music room.

They played a little popular duet first, then switched to nursery rhymes for the child's sake. They started with "Three Blind Mice" and when it was finished, Amy looked at Mollie in horror.

"Cut off their tails with a carving knife?" She repeated the lyrics.

I never realized it was so bloody! That's awful. Let's change the words."
 And so they fiddled with the song for a while and laughingly came up with a less violent version.

No matter what they played, Jaime danced to it. He loved to dance.

"Not like his father," Mollie laughed. "He really doesn't like to dance much. Now his grandfather, Jimmy Fitzgerald, may he rest in peace, he was a fine dancer."

She looked wistful and was quiet for a moment.

Amy placed her hand on Mollie's.

"Tell me about Rory's father," she urged.

Mollie brightened and began to describe him.

"He was a rogue, for sure," she said, laughing. "He swept me off my feet first time I met him. He could laugh like nobody I've ever known. Liked the whisky, but was never a mean drunk. Always with the joke, my Jimmy."

Mollie sobered and looked at Amy.

"And, praise the saints, the only thing Rory got from his father was his handsome looks and his size—and an occasional indulgence in his temper," she said.

Her pride in her son was evident. But she was realistic about his father.

"Jimmy Fitzgerald was not a good husband, nor a good father," she said. "He was all about adventuring and having a good time. Rory and I paid for that. He was seldom there for us, and when he died, I heard lots of stories about him. I wasn't the only woman in his life. You've heard the phrase, 'a girl in every port'? Well, that was Jimmy."

Amy hugged Mollie on impulse. Jamie came running over to join the hug—he still loved hugging.

When Mollie sat back, she had tears in her eyes.

"What you need to know is that Rory is nothing like that. He's faithful and loyal to everyone in his life. He's a hard worker and he never lets his friends or family down. He's nothing like his father in those ways.

"Oh he does have a bit of mischief in him at times—I could tell you stories about pranks he pulled on his friends and cousins growing up. But he doesn't have a mean bone in his body. He'd be so good to you and Jamie."

Amy sat back, looking at the woman who could have, under the right circumstances, become her mother-in-law.

"I need to find out who I am and what I am capable of before I commit myself to any man," Amy said. "I hope you understand that. I care for Rory more than I can say, but I spent my whole life until recently under the control of someone else. I want to find out who Amy is."

Mollie smiled.

"Darlin'," she said, "I totally agree with that. I didn't find my own path until after Jimmy died. At first, I thought I would have to remarry in order to live. Then Rory's grandfather, old Ronan Fitzgerald, put me to work in the company. At first, I think it was a token job, so I could support myself and my son. He knew I was too independent to just live off him.

"Before long, he realized I had a brain of my own and that I was an asset to the business. I worked my way up and became the person on whom he most depended.

"When Rory reached his majority and finished his education, he came into the business full time. He had sailed with several of our ships in the summers, but was a quick learner and it wasn't long before he became a captain. He earned it, too. When he wasn't collecting new clients for the shipping business, that is."

Mollie was pensive for a few moments.

"As a ship's captain," she continued, "he was well liked and ruled not by brutality, as many have, but by earning the admiration and respect of his crew. They're all loyal to him to a fault. As he is to them."

Amy responded.

"I can tell that from the few crew members I have met," she said. "Loyalty is a precious thing, and the fact that he inspires it says a lot about him as a man."

She looked directly at Mollie.

"I am aware of all his good qualities, but you must know that my refusal to marry him is no reflection upon him. It's a reflection of what I need to do at this point in my life. I don't want to make the wrong decision for the wrong reasons—for him or for me."

Mollie hugged the girl again, and at Jamie's insistence began to play "Little Boy Blue."

But the conversation lingered in both their minds.

After that, Amy felt closer than ever to Mollie.

She spent many mornings writing her "memoir" of being a lightkeeper, hoping Mr. Harkness would like it. She had fun learning to master the new typing machine. She spent afternoons at the shipping office, and the rest of the time taking care of, and enjoying time with, her son. She noticed she was not seeing as much of Rory these days and tried not to let it bother her. But it did.

Mollie distracted her with a day of shopping, during which Amy admired many things but bought nothing for herself. Then Aunt Bridget did the same thing. They stopped by the dressmaker's for a final fitting for a summer frock Aunt Bridget had ordered.

Once again, Amy admired the goods—especially a supple cream silk fabric—but bought herself nothing.

One evening, when Rory was very late coming home, Uncle Seamus came into the library and sat with her and Jamie. He told her another lightkeeper story he had heard, about a woman who kept dozens of cats for company at her solitary post, and who swore her cats could predict the weather. Word had it that she took up fishing just to feed them.

"I can fish," Amy told him when the story was over.

Uncle Seamus' bushy brows rose almost to his forehead.

"You can fish?" he responded, as if he had not heard her right.

"Yes, Charlie taught me how to fish at Point Peril," she replied. "It was a nice change from salted meat provided by the lighthouse service. If I never see another piece of salted pork, it will still be too soon."

They both laughed.

"I had enough of that slag when I was at sea," Seamus said. "I agree heartily."

Then he asked her if she really could swim.

"I can," Amy said, not without pride. "I taught myself that, too, so my form isn't proper, but I can stay afloat."

"Well, it was good enough to save my nephew's life," he said. "We'll all be forever grateful to you for that."

Amy smiled at him and leaned over to squeeze his hand.

"And it brought me to all of you, for which I am truly grateful," she replied.

Seamus grinned in embarrassment, then cleared his throat and asked Jamie if he wanted to take a run in the garden before bed.

Jamie nodded happily and took Seamus' hand as they left the library.

Amy realized she would dearly miss living in close proximity to these people. It would be hard on Jamie, too. It was likely he did not remember his mostly solitary first year of life with his mother, and this family was all he had known since then.

One morning in mid-May, when Amy came in to breakfast with Jamie, the dining room was deserted. That seemed odd. Usually, *someone* was there. She went to the sideboard and discovered all her least favorite dishes—fish poached in milk, sautéed chicken livers and hard-boiled eggs.

She decided Mrs. Flannery must be in a snit about something, or had taken sick. She took some toast and tea for herself and toast with an egg for Jamie and was about to sit down when the door to the dining room burst open and everyone was there—Rory, Bridget and Seamus, Mollie, Susan and Mrs. Flannery, shouting "Happy birthday!"

Mrs. Flannery was carrying a platter with Amy's favorite —a pile of light, fluffy pancakes sauced with fresh fruit and topped with whipped cream so rich it looked like butter. Jamie clapped his hands. It was his favorite, too.

"How did you know it was my birthday?" Amy asked, after their good wishes died down.

"Your mother told us when they were here last," Mollie said. "We promised not to forget."

They all sat down to eat. Uncle Seamus loved the poached fish and sautéed livers but almost everyone else chose the pancakes, so Mrs. Flannery headed back into the kitchen to make more.

It was a festive breakfast and Rory informed her that she could just relax, because she was not going to work that day.

"I have other plans for you," he said, cryptically.

Mollie presented her with a lovely silk shawl they had eyed on their shopping excursion. Amy knew it was scandalously expensive, but Mollie shushed her protests. Bridget presented her with a dressmaker's box that contained the most gorgeous cream-colored summer frock she had ever seen, with a froth of lace along the V-shaped neckline and another at the hem. Of course, the dressmaker already had her measurements, and Amy had admired this very same cream silk fabric on their shopping trip.

Jamie ran to Susan who gave him something, and he ran back to his mother with a nosegay of fresh flowers from the garden.

"Thank you, darling," she said, kissing her son, who wiggled with delight.

"Smell!" he urged her, and she did, giving an appreciative sniff. "Pwetty fwowers," he informed the group.

"You are all so wonderful," she said, smiling at each of them and looking not-too-expectantly, she hoped, at Rory.

"You'll have to wait for later for my gift," he said. "Why don't you get dressed in something for an outing and lunch at a fine restaurant?" he suggested. "I'll fetch you in an hour."

Amy, Jamie and Susan returned to the cottage, where Susan helped her unbraid her hair and style it more fashionably. She put on her best day dress, a soft blue muslin, and was glad the mermaid pendant showed in the neckline.

Rory was out front promptly in one hour and helped Amy into an open carriage. It was a fine day, and she had added her new silk shawl just in case. A light straw bonnet kept her hair in place. She was ready.

Lunch at a fine restaurant would be a nice treat, indeed, but what would they do from now till lunchtime, she wondered.

They headed not toward the tree-lined lanes or even to the shops of Boston, but to the shipyards. Amy was puzzled. Maybe Rory had some business to attend to on the way? He ignored her curious glances and he actually seemed nervous. She had never seen him nervous. He was always so confident, composed and calm—except on the rare occasion when he lost his temper.

They stopped short of entering the shipyard. Rory asked her to close her eyes.

"Why?" Amy asked. "What for?"

"So as not to spoil the surprise," Rory replied. "Please. Just close your eyes."

Amy complied, and he drove on a short way, then stopped.

"Before you open your eyes, I want to say something," Rory said. Instead, he kissed her. Taken by surprise, Amy's eyes flew open. As Rory pulled away from her she saw it: the most beautiful ship she had ever seen. The graceful, almost sensuous lines, were a work of art. Its gleaming sails, furled but new and clean, the glow of the wood, the shine of the brass fittings, were all stunning.

Then her gaze swept to the bow, where a woman's figurehead pressed forward, as if ready to embrace the sea. The head segued into a mermaid's body, which blended into the prow of the ship seamlessly. The mermaid's hair flowed over her breasts and stomach. And beside the figurehead was the ship's name: *The Mermaid*.

But what caught Amy off guard most was the face of the mermaid. It was her face. The face from Rory's sketch book.

She was speechless. Rory watched her intently.

"Happy birthday, sweetheart," he said. "I built her in honor of you."

Amy stared silently at the ship, unable to speak.

"Say something," he prompted her.

"Oh, Rory," she whispered. "It's the most beautiful thing I've ever seen. I don't know what to say! And is that really me, naked on the prow?"

Rory threw his head back and laughed.

"It is indeed! I hope you're not offended. It was meant as a compliment."

So this is what all the secrecy was about—hiding the portfolio and its drawings, disappearing for long days at a time. She was overwhelmed with it. No one had ever done anything like this to impress her—ever.

"I really don't know what to say," she said, and for some reason felt like crying.

Rory took both of her hands and looked into her eyes.

"Say you'll marry me," he said.

Amy closed her eyes and mustered all the willpower.

"You know why I can't," she replied. "We've been over this."

"But you saved my life," Rory said.

"I did my job," Amy replied.

"You bore me a son," he said.

"And that's as much my fault as yours," she came back.

"We like the same things," he said.

"Yes, we do, but liking the same things isn't reason enough to marry."

"My family adores you."

"And I adore them. And Jamie does, too."

"Jamie needs brothers and sisters."

"Yes, he does, but I can marry someone else. And you would not have to be giving up your life at sea.

Rory took a deep breath.

"You are NOT marrying anyone else. And I am NOT going back to sea," he said.

"I can't ask you to give that up," Amy protested.

"You're not. I'm giving it up because ... and please don't tell anyone else ... because I get seasick."

Amy's eyes widened.

"What? When did this happen? How?"

"Ever since my head injury, I get seasick on the high seas," he said. "Only Uncle Seamus knows. Oh, I can do an easy sail along the coast for a few hours, but anything more than that leaves me violently ill. The doctor said it's likely it would never go away."

Amy felt a rush of relief in her chest, like she could breathe again after holding her breath for a long, long time. Like she had just been rescued from drowning. She kind of knew what that felt like.

"We can have a normal life" Rory continued. "And I've found that my real passion isn't being a sea captain. It's building ships. I want to draw and design ships for others, too. *The Mermaid* will be my example to show off to the world. She's a beauty, isn't she? Just like my Amy."

But Amy wouldn't be put off with compliments.

"Won't you miss going to sea?" she asked.

"I've found something I like better," Rory said. "I like designing and building ships. I like evenings with you and Jamie. I like having a home life. And I'm not asking you to marry me out of obligation or duty.

"I am asking you to marry me because you are the most amazing woman I have ever known. You are beautiful and strong and a wonderful mother. You are kind and so smart it scares me sometimes.

"You are no simpering, eyelash-fluttering debutante. You are a woman of integrity, who knows her own mind. You are the kind of woman any man should want as a partner in life. To share his bed, to raise his children, to explore the world. And I love you with all my heart."

Amy felt the tears coming. These were all the things that spoke to her heart. And he had finally expressed them so eloquently.

"Oh, Rory, I love you, too, and denying you all this time has been the hardest thing I have ever done. Yes, I will marry you. We will have a wonderful life together, I just know it. More children, I hope.

"But there's just one thing."

"Anything," Rory said, pulling her close for a kiss. "What is it?"

"I still want to write my book," she said.

"Fine by me," he said, and kissed her forehead.

"Oh, and another thing. I still want to keep my own bank account," she said.

He laughed and kissed her nose.

"Not a problem," he said.

"Oh, and I would like to have my own office," she said, wondering if she was going too far.

"As long as you share my bed, you can have the rest of the house for all I care," he said, kissing her on both cheeks.

"And I want to be married at Port Smythe, at the lighthouse," she added.

Rory sat back and looked at her.

"Darlin', we could be married in a dinghy if you want. As long as it's tied up to a dock and the sea is calm."

He kissed her properly then, and she kissed him back. It brought whistles from some of the shipyard workers, who laughed and clapped their hands, as if they knew what was going on.

Amy didn't care. Her heart was singing, and she was as happy as she had ever been in her whole life.

Rory was elated.

"I didn't bring a ring, just in case it jinxed the proposal," he said.

"I don't need a ring," Amy said. "I have everything I could ever want right now."

It was hard to drive to lunch with both arms wrapped around her, but he managed.

The family celebrated not only her birthday, but the engagement that night at dinner. Mrs. Flannery went all out with roasted lamb chops and new potatoes, plus fresh spring asparagus from the garden. An elaborate birthday cake topped off the meal. That part was by far Jamie's favorite, and he fell asleep at the table with frosting on his face.

After dinner, Rory carried the boy back to the cottage, and they put him to bed, wiping his face with a warm, wet cloth. Rory slipped his arm around her waist, and she put her head on his shoulder as they stared down at their son.

"I can't wait to make a half dozen more just like him," he whispered to her. Amy laughed and said, "A half dozen? Are you sure?"

"Well, we created him in one night. We will have lots of nights together, once we are married. Unless you want to start now?"

"Oh, don't tempt me, sir!" she cried, playing at being coy. Then she sobered. "I want nothing more."

He led her to the bed in the next room. He lay beside her and they kissed for a while, then Rory raised up on one elbow.

"Lord knows, I won't sleep tonight, but if I do, it will be to dream of you being next to me soon."

When he left, if was like half of her had been torn away.

She finally got up to get ready for bed, and on her dresser she found a box with a simple gold ring studded with tiny diamonds like stars. It was perfect, exactly what she would have chosen for herself.

A note inside said, simply: "For our wedding day."

CHAPTER FIFTEEN

In the weeks leading up to the wedding, Amy found herself vacillating between excitement and nervousness. She knew she loved Rory, and she knew Jamie loved him, too. She adored his family and they seemed to reciprocate. She had gained his assurance that he would support her writing venture and, if it worked out, possibly even some proofreading work for Mr. Harkness. They planned to travel together to gather stories for her book and for him to show off his ship to potential customers. As long as they stayed close to shore and in calm waters, he said.

The only thing that really worried her was how she would be accepted into Boston society. It was not something that normally might bother her, but she realized that she knew very few people outside the Fitzgerald family and employees. Would she be expected to socialize with the family's friends and business associates? Rory seldom did. He was invited to everything but attended few things. Mollie, on the other hand, was active in that world. She often used her impressive charm to garner business deals.

Would people look askance at their quiet marriage?

What would happen when everyone realized she had given birth to Rory's son out of wedlock? It bothered her, frankly, that these things bothered her. But they did. She did not want to embarrass any of them, especially her husband-to-be.

The test came soon. Aunt Bridget and Mollie organized a women's tea party on a Saturday afternoon and invited a number of women they knew. Some were older—Mollie's friends, mostly—and some were young matrons closer to Amy's age. And there were a few younger women, just coming out in society, too.

Amy wasn't fooled by the casual tea party setting. She had witnessed enough of her mother's gatherings to know that her behavior could make or break her reputation with these women.

Amy decided to wear a simple aquamarine gown and to put her long hair up into a chignon for the occasion. She wore her mermaid medallion—by far her favorite piece of jewelry.

Mollie and Aunt Bridget approved of her choices, and complimented her to boost her confidence.

"They're just going to eat you up!" Aunt Bridget declared, hugging her.

"As long as they don't eat me alive," Amy retorted, caution coloring her voice.

The day dawned flawlessly, so the party was held in the garden, which had enough shade to protect even the most milky-white skin.

Amy stood with Mollie and greeted guests while Aunt Bridget made sure the kitchen ran smoothly and service was elegant.

She was dismayed to see Dorothy O'Donnell (or Dottie

the Debutante, as she had dubbed her), but greeted her as pleasantly as the rest. Dottie simpered off to join some of her young, unmarried friends at one table. Amy ended up sitting with the young matrons, who had saved her a spot.

Several of them seemed quite nice and interesting, and she was soon engaged in listening to their conversation. One bit of gossip did catch her attention.

"Our Reverend Jonathan Snead has been at it again," said one woman. "He's tried courting every eligible young woman of means in the entire city, I think, but most of their fathers have driven him off. He's such a transparent gold-digger!"

Several other women chimed in with stories about the greedy minister, but Amy kept her own counsel. She'd have to tell Rory about his romantic antics later, though.

She offered little about herself unless asked directly, as was her habit. She didn't mention her unconventional stint as a lightkeeper until one of the women asked her, a bit hesitantly, if it was true she had been employed thusly.

If Amy was reluctant to talk about her past experiences to these women, she also was never anything but forthright.

"I was indeed a lightkeeper for a time," she admitted. And this set off a flurry of questions. Most of the women were fascinated by her experiences and wanted to know more. A few seemed taken aback by the confession, but still intrigued. Eventually, Amy became less shy. They thought she was interesting!

She was just getting comfortable with her group when Rory entered the garden, looking around. He was supposed to be at the shipyard this afternoon, she thought. He had cleaned up, changed into a fine coat and breeches, and tamed his wayward wavy copper hair into a tidy queue. He looked so handsome. She felt a little thrill when he spotted her and broke into a broad smile. He headed straight in her direction.

"Oh, Captain Fitzgerald," Dottie gushed, grabbing his sleeve as he passed. She giggled flirtatiously. "How brave of you to venture into a women's tea party!"

Her young friends giggled, too, as Rory stopped briefly, said hello, then gently but firmly removed her restraining hand.

"Excuse me," he said, politely, "but I got home early and could not wait to say hello to my bride-to-be."

Dottie's mouth dropped open in a most unladylike expression as he stopped in front of Amy, made a small bow, took her hand and kissed it. As he bent over her hand, he glanced at her and gave her a wink. Amy blushed, but it was with pleasure, not embarrassment. The ladies at the party all began to chatter excitedly and call out congratulations. Several of them even rushed over to hug Amy.

"But this is wonderful!" said one.

"About time someone caught the eye of this rogue," teased another.

Suddenly, the party took on a celebratory air.

"If you ask me, it's a very unusual way to announce an engagement," Dottie said, quite loudly.

One of Aunt Bridget's friends gave the girl a cold stare.

"Young lady," she said, reprovingly, "I don't believe anyone asked you."

Dottie's cheeks flamed, and she fell silent.

Amy was unaware of most of this, because she only had eyes for Rory. He had honored her and simultaneously made their engagement announcement in front of the most powerful force in Boston society: its women.

Rory ordered champagne to be brought out along with more tea, and it truly became a party. He never left Amy's side.

That night, as he walked her to the garden cottage, she thanked him for it.

"I thought it might help smooth the way for you," he said. "But you didn't need me. They loved you."

Amy looked up at him, his features and unruly hair burnished by the full moon's glow.

"That's one hurdle down, and another to go," she said.

"What's the other hurdle?" he asked. But he knew.

"Jamie," she replied. "As soon as they meet him, they'll know he's your son. They're not all as well educated as you and I, but I think they can figure out that he was born long before the wedding. How will that change things?"

He smoothed her hair and kissed her gently.

"Sweetheart," he said. "These can be fickle folk. They've already fallen in love with you. I believe they like and respect me. When they figure it out, there'll be some tittering behind hands and a few raised eyebrows, but they'll forgive just about anything if it's convenient for them to do so. And I'll make sure it is. So will my mother."

He held her for a while and she sighed.

"I think you might be right, but it's too bad that if I were a shrew and you were a boor, and didn't have money and influence, our child would suffer for it."

"A shrew and a boor?" Rory repeated. "My, my you do paint an enticing picture of us!"

She slapped him playfully.

"You know what I mean," she laughed.

"I do," he admitted. "But once you earn people's affection and respect, they're a lot more likely to look the other way at an indiscretion. Especially when we marry. And besides, I plan to adopt Jamie legally as soon as we are wed. If that's all right with you, that is."

Amy smiled and stood on tiptoe to kiss him, more ardently this time.

"It's more than all right with me," she said. "It's perfect."

He returned her ardent kiss, finally pulled away reluctantly and said goodnight.

"Sweet Jesus," he muttered to himself as he walked away. "I can't wait for our wedding night."

Amy heard him and smiled.

THEY HAD SETTLED ON A JUNE WEDDING. They couldn't wait much longer, they decided. Rory's grandfather was due to arrive around the first of the month for a visit. He had been wanting to meet her and his great-grandson and had planned the trip before the engagement was official.

Amy wrote to her parents, and to Charlie and Bess, and told them all the news. They would take *The Mermaid* on her maiden voyage down to Port Smythe and dock her, get married at the lighthouse, and everyone would stay at the Harbor Inn.

Everyone except Amy and Rory, who would spend their wedding night in the plush captain's cabin of the ship, safely anchored in port. That would give them privacy and, he promised her, they would need lots of privacy.

Amy shivered with anticipation, recalling the night of the storm. If the marriage bed was half as exciting as that night, she could hardly wait. And she suspected it might even surpass her expectations, dealing with a man who was fully conscious this time.

But first, she took time to take stock of her meager possessions and decide what to do with them. There wasn't much. She took out of her little trunk a framed photo of Reuben, her first husband. His face barely seemed familiar to her now. He stood, stiff and proud, in his Union soldier's uniform. It seemed like a lifetime ago that he left for the war. She would send the photo to his parents, who had become quite reclusive since his death. Perhaps it would comfort them, somehow.

Gently, she lifted a stiff envelope from the trunk. Inside was a silhouette of her sweet baby girl. She had let an artist do it at a summer fair when her daughter was only 2. Though it was only an outline, her memory filled in the tiny features without hesitation. She pressed it to her heart, then returned it to the envelope, and laid it carefully in the trunk.

She took a deep breath and returned to practical matters. Her rocking chair and writing desk would easily find space in her new home, as would the baby pen—for future use, she hoped.

She didn't have many possessions, but what she did have was a self-assurance she had not had before she got her job as a lightkeeper. How much she had learned! How far she had come! She no longer recognized the girl who broke out of grief to make a new life for herself. And she liked this new person.

And now she had another life waiting for her. And a wedding to look forward to.

As they set off on their wedding journey, Jamie was beside himself with excitement as they walked up the gangplank to the ship. He almost literally bounced onto the deck. Rory kept a close eye on him.

Aunt Bridget and Uncle Seamus sailed with them, along with Susan, to help keep Jamie in tow. Mollie and the newly arrived Ronan Fitzgerald took a carriage. He'd just been at sea for weeks and was ready for some land travel. The elder Fitzgerald took to Amy and Jamie as if he'd known them all his life. And they to him. He took one look at little Jamie and then at his grandson, and laughed.

"No guessing who his father is!" he said.

Cousin Thomas was riding his horse and would meet them there. Her parents also would meet them at the inn.

When they arrived in Port Smythe, they all checked into the Harbor Inn. Amy spent the night with Mollie, and Rory bunked with his grandfather. It would be their last night apart.

Amy couldn't wait to see Charlie and Bess, and she didn't have to. They were waiting on the pier when the ship docked. Bess rushed forward to hug Amy. Charlie shuffled his feet in embarrassment and finally allowed himself to be hugged, too. Charlie had made another small wooden toy for Jamie —a wooden lighthouse, complete with a catwalk around the topmost level.

Jamie didn't really remember the older couple, but yet seemed to find them familiar. After all, he hadn't seen them for ten months—a lifetime to a little one. But he was soon won over by the wooden toy and Bess' cookies.

Rory had arranged for the new minister at the little church to officiate, giving him a nice "donation" to come do the ceremony at the lighthouse. He was a sweet, elderly man who didn't seem to mind performing a somewhat unorthodox ceremony.

The next morning dawned bright and clear, a perfect June

day. Amy dressed in the creamy silk and lace confection Aunt Bridget had given her for her birthday. She wore her waist-length hair down, brushed till it shone like a sheet of dark silk, and a circlet of flowers on her head. Rory had reclaimed the ring in its box for the ceremony.

Everyone was dressed in their finery as they gathered at the lighthouse. Jeremiah came out to greet them, also dressed in his Sunday best, and hugged Amy as though she were a long-lost sister. Rory noticed with pride that everyone loved her, but he thought Thomas hugged her just a bit too often and too long. He'd have to have a talk with him about that.

Just as they were beginning to start the ceremony, they heard a visitor arriving. It was Mrs. Agatha Bean, urging her pony to go faster. They waited for her to dismount and rush over to the group, red-faced and panting.

"I'm sorry to be arriving uninvited, but I just couldn't miss this," she explained, catching her breath. "Bless you both! This is just so romantic!"

Amy hugged her and told her it was fine, that she was glad to have her there. Mrs. Bean beamed.

Then Amy walked over to Rory, took his hand and looked up at him.

"I think it's time," she said.

"And about damned time," Uncle Seamus muttered.

The ceremony was short and simple, after which they all returned to their hired carriages to go back to the Harbor Inn for a wedding dinner. Mrs. Bean was invited to join them and gladly accepted.

Amy wasn't sure what she ate. Her heart was so full, it seemed it would burst.

Thomas announced at dinner that he was moving back

to Ireland to serve an apprenticeship with Ronan Fitzgerald, to learn more about the shipping business from the Irish side. Rory smiled a little secret smile to himself, but Amy saw it and knew what he'd been up to.

After a lingering dinner, and a toast or two, she followed Charlie, Bess and Jeremiah outside to say their farewells.

"How's the lighthouse keeping?" she asked the young man.

"It's a great life," Jeremiah said. "It's a good job and I don't have to be stuck in a smelly old blacksmith's shop all day. Besides, I got me a girl now and am asking her to marry me. She thinks the lighthouse is the most romantic place ever to live. Afraid she might not think so after a while, but for now it's just fine."

He said Matilda the cat was still good company, but had borne no more kittens.

"Guess she's gettin' past her prime," he said.

Charlie and Bess both gave her extra hugs, and Amy assured them she'd see them again soon. They were an important part of her life, and she would not let their friendship fade. She'd bring Jamie to see them often.

She spent part of the afternoon visiting with her parents, who would head home the next day.

"I'm so happy for you," her mother said. "He's such a handsome rogue! And he is so good with Jamie. Anyone can see he's wild about you."

Her father was fascinated about the book she was writing. Mr. Harkness had given her the go-ahead to keep working on it.

"Always knew you were too smart for just housekeeping," he said.

"Not that housekeeping isn't a worthwhile pursuit," he added to mollify his wife, who was giving him dark looks.

"Anyway, I'm very proud of you, my dear. I can't wait to read the book."

As evening neared, Amy and Rory kept casting each other longing looks to the point where everyone else pretended to want an early night, so the couple could leave.

They chose to walk down to the dock, just a short distance away, to *The Mermaid*. As they entered the captain's cabin, Amy saw flowers that had not been there before. A small bottle of champagne chilled on a table. A bowl of fresh strawberries glistened in the candle light.

"Oh, Rory, you thought of everything," she said. "You'll spoil me—and then where will you be when I become one of those simpering females you say you so despise?"

"Never," he said, taking her in his arms. He kissed her fervently.

But there was one more delay.

"Can we go up on deck for a moment?" Amy asked.

"I'll make love to you anywhere you want," he said, nuzzling her neck.

"Soon," she promised. "I just want to take one last look at the lighthouse, all lit up for the night."

They went back up on deck and walked to the captain's perch. They stood there, looking at the light.

"It was what guided me to safety the night of the storm," Rory said. "It gave me hope and direction. Like you have given my life now.

"And, after all," he teased her once more. "You did save my life."

Amy turned to him and kissed him tenderly on the lips.

Then she stood by his side, wound her fingers through his and laid her head on his shoulder.

"No," she said, disagreeing with him gently. "I believe it was you who saved mine."

ACKNOWLEDGMENTS

Thanks go to my writer's group—Marty Banks, Maria Faulconer, Toni Knapp, and Susan Rust, who spent many hours reading first drafts and offering thoughtful suggestions while I was writing this book.

Also, thanks go to my husband Rick, for his supprt throughout the process.

ABOUT THE AUTHOR

Linda DuVal holds a bachelor's degree in English and was an award-winning reporter, feature writer, and section editor at The Gazette in Colorado Springs for 32 years. She is now a freelance writer. She lives in Colorado Springs with her husband, Rick.

Printed in the USA
CPSIA information can be obtained
at www.ICGtesting.com
JSHW022041030224
56290JS00003B/30

9 781943 829538